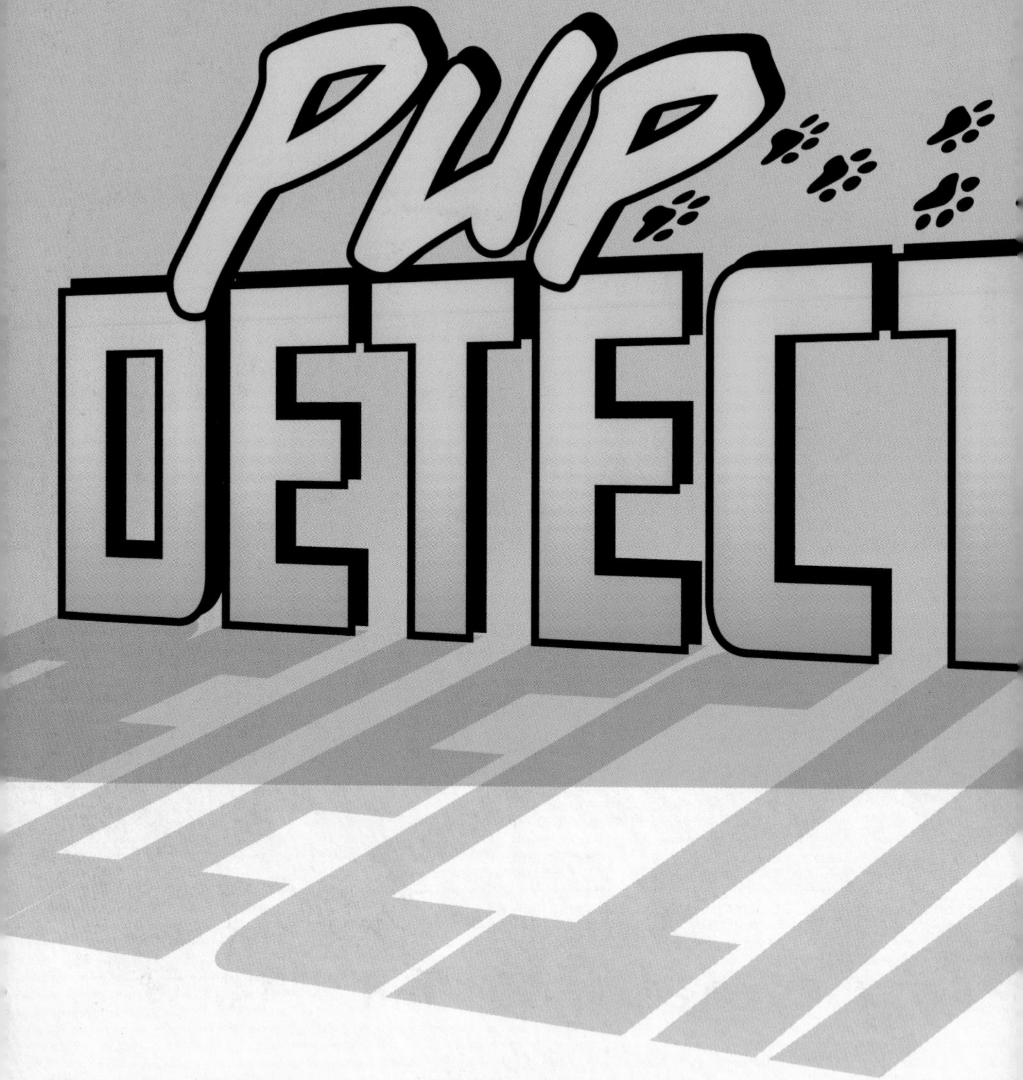
PUP
DETECT

MYSTERY MOUNTAIN GETAWAY

Written by **FELIX GUMPAW**
Illustrated by **WALMIR ARCHANJO**
at **GLASS HOUSE GRAPHICS**

LITTLE SIMON
NEW YORK LONDON TORONTO SYDNEY NEW DELHI

LITTLE SIMON
AN IMPRINT OF SIMON & SCHUSTER CHILDREN'S PUBLISHING DIVISION
1230 AVENUE OF THE AMERICAS, NEW YORK, NEW YORK 10020
FIRST LITTLE SIMON EDITION OCTOBER 2021
COPYRIGHT © 2021 BY SIMON & SCHUSTER, INC.
ALL RIGHTS RESERVED, INCLUDING THE RIGHT OF REPRODUCTION IN WHOLE OR IN PART IN ANY FORM. LITTLE SIMON IS A REGISTERED TRADEMARK OF SIMON & SCHUSTER, INC., AND ASSOCIATED COLOPHON IS A TRADEMARK OF SIMON & SCHUSTER, INC. FOR INFORMATION ABOUT SPECIAL DISCOUNTS FOR BULK PURCHASES, PLEASE CONTACT SIMON & SCHUSTER SPECIAL SALES AT 1-866-506-1949 OR BUSINESS@SIMONANDSCHUSTER.COM. ART BY WALMIR ARCHANJO AND JOAO MARIO TEIXEIRA DE ARAUJO • COLORING BY WALMIR ARCHANJO AND RAFAEL RAMOS • LETTERING BY MARCOS MASSAO INOUE • SUPERVISION BY MJ MACEDO/STUPLENDO • ART SERVICES BY GLASS HOUSE GRAPHICS • THE SIMON & SCHUSTER SPEAKERS BUREAU CAN BRING AUTHORS TO YOUR LIVE EVENT. FOR MORE INFORMATION OR TO BOOK AN EVENT CONTACT THE SIMON & SCHUSTER SPEAKERS BUREAU AT 1-866-248-3049 OR VISIT OUR WEBSITE AT WWW.SIMONSPEAKERS.COM.
DESIGNED BY NICHOLAS SCIACCA
MANUFACTURED IN CHINA 0821 SCP
10 9 8 7 6 5 4 3 2 1
LIBRARY OF CONGRESS CATALOGING-IN-PUBLICATION DATA
NAMES: GUMPAW, FELIX, AUTHOR. I GLASS HOUSE GRAPHICS, ILLUSTRATOR.
TITLE: MYSTERY MOUNTAIN GETAWAY / BY FELIX GUMPAW ; ILLUSTRATED BY GLASS HOUSE GRAPHICS. DESCRIPTION: FIRST LITTLE SIMON EDITION. I NEW YORK : LITTLE SIMON, 2021. I SERIES: PUP DETECTIVES ; 6 I AUDIENCE: AGES 5-9 I AUDIENCE: GRADES K-1 I SUMMARY: WHEN RIDER WOOFSON AND THE P.I. PACK ARRIVE AT THE TOP OF MYSTERY MOUNTAIN, THEY FIND THEIR CLASSMATES HAVE LEFT, SCARED AWAY BY A SNOW MONSTER, SO THE DETECTIVES DECIDE IT IS TIME TO INVESTIGATE EXACTLY WHAT IS SO MYSTERIOUS ABOUT THIS MOUNTAIN. IDENTIFIERS: LCCN 2020049152 (PRINT) I LCCN 2020049153 (EBOOK) I ISBN 9781534484870 (PAPERBACK) I ISBN 9781534484887 (HARDCOVER) I ISBN 9781534484894 (EBOOK). SUBJECTS: LCSH: GRAPHIC NOVELS. I CYAC: GRAPHIC NOVELS. I MYSTERY AND DETECTIVE STORIES. I DOGS–FICTION. CLASSIFICATION: LCC PZ7.7.G858 MY 2021 (PRINT) I LCC PZ7.7.G858 (EBOOK) IDDC 741.5/973–DC23. LC RECORD AVAILABLE AT HTTPS://LCCN.LOC.GOV/2020049152. LC EBOOK RECORD AVAILABLE AT HTTPS://LCCN.LOC.GOV/2020049153

CONTENTS

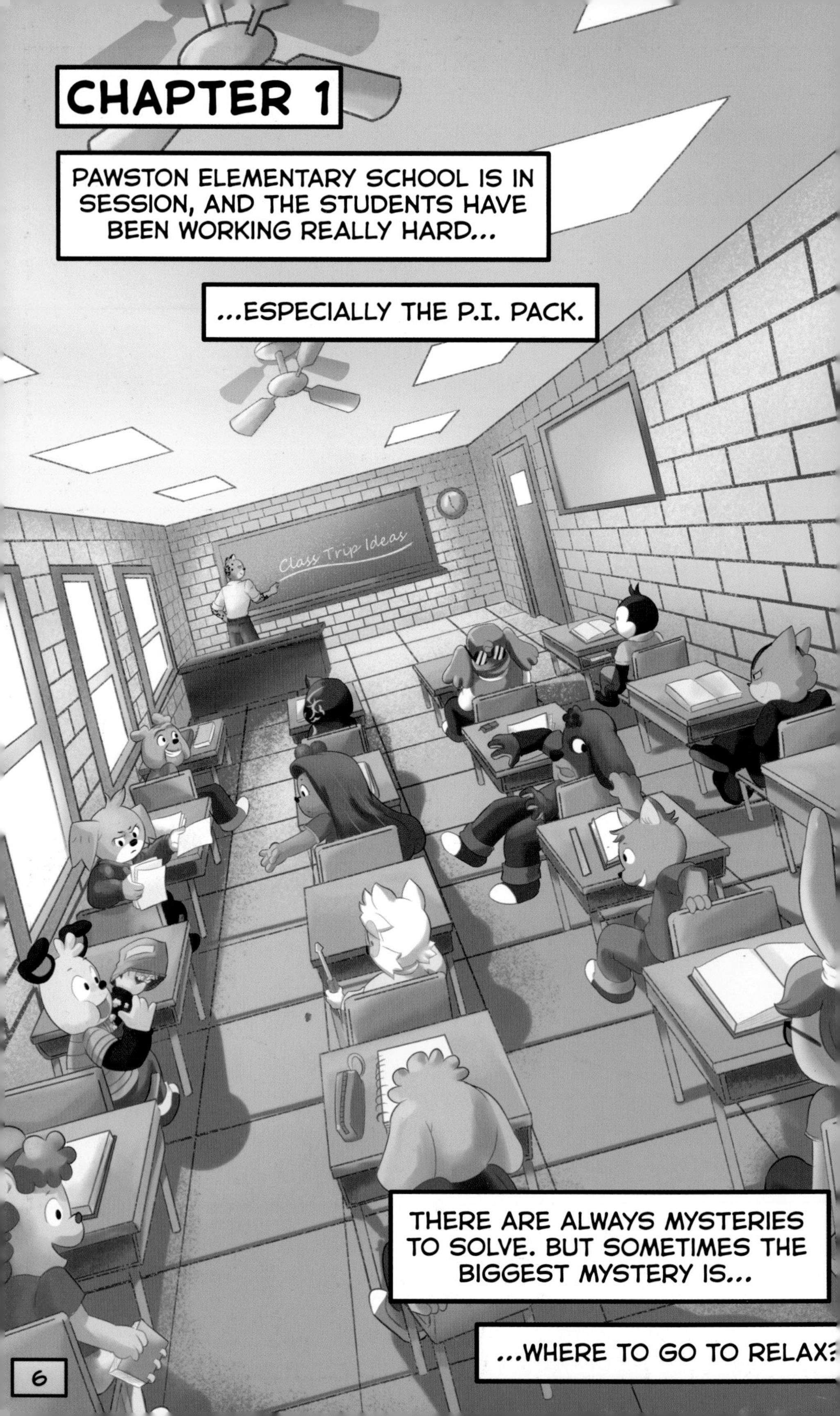
CHAPTER 1
PAWSTON ELEMENTARY SCHOOL IS IN SESSION, AND THE STUDENTS HAVE BEEN WORKING REALLY HARD...
...ESPECIALLY THE P.I. PACK.
Class Trip Ideas
THERE ARE ALWAYS MYSTERIES TO SOLVE. BUT SOMETIMES THE BIGGEST MYSTERY IS...
...WHERE TO GO TO RELAX?

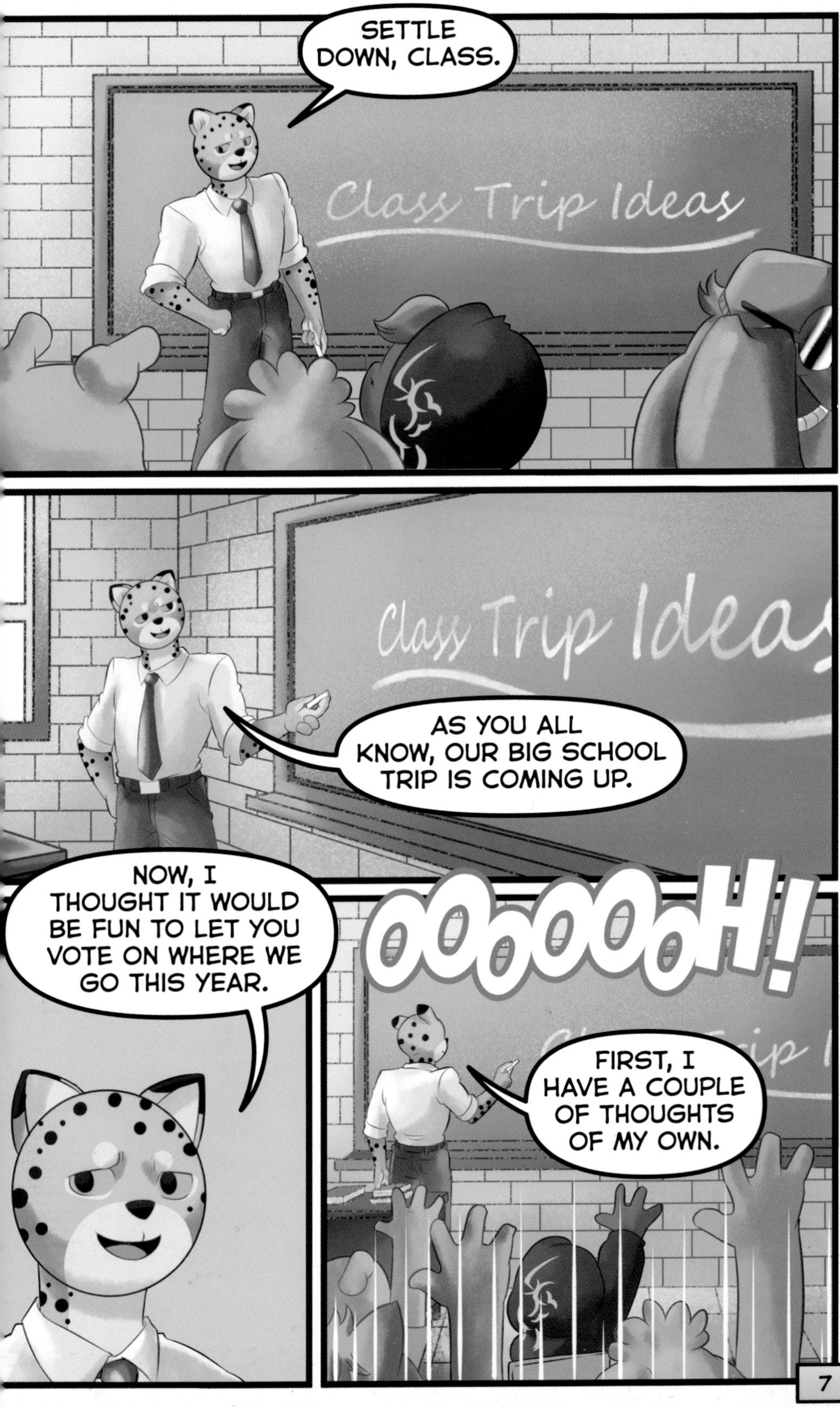
SETTLE DOWN, CLASS.
Class Trip Ideas
Class Trip Ideas
AS YOU ALL KNOW, OUR BIG SCHOOL TRIP IS COMING UP.
NOW, I THOUGHT IT WOULD BE FUN TO LET YOU VOTE ON WHERE WE GO THIS YEAR.
OOOOOOOH!
FIRST, I HAVE A COUPLE OF THOUGHTS OF MY OWN.

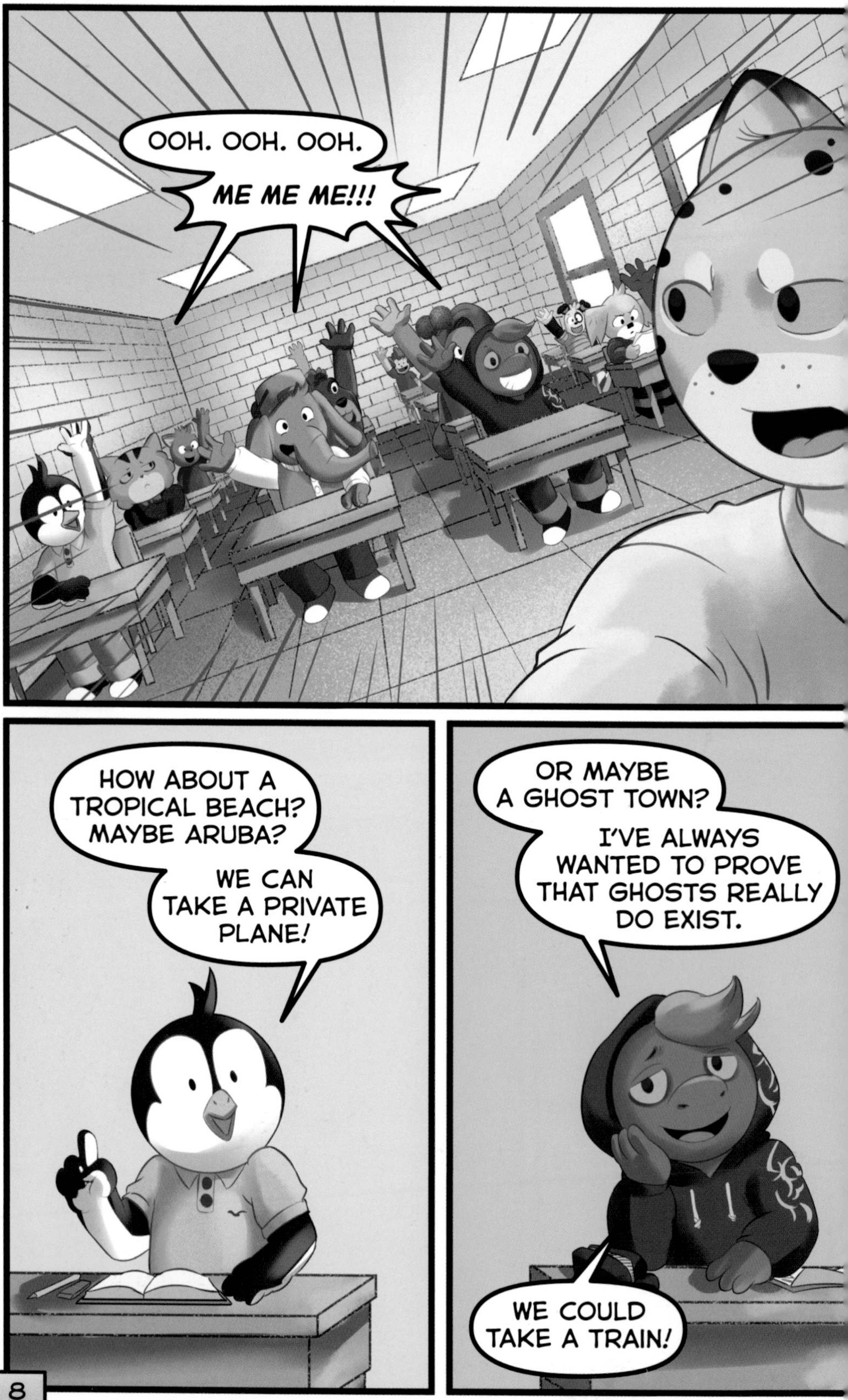
OOH. OOH. OOH.
ME ME ME!!!
HOW ABOUT A TROPICAL BEACH? MAYBE ARUBA?
WE CAN TAKE A PRIVATE PLANE!
OR MAYBE A GHOST TOWN?
I'VE ALWAYS WANTED TO PROVE THAT GHOSTS REALLY DO EXIST.
WE COULD TAKE A TRAIN!

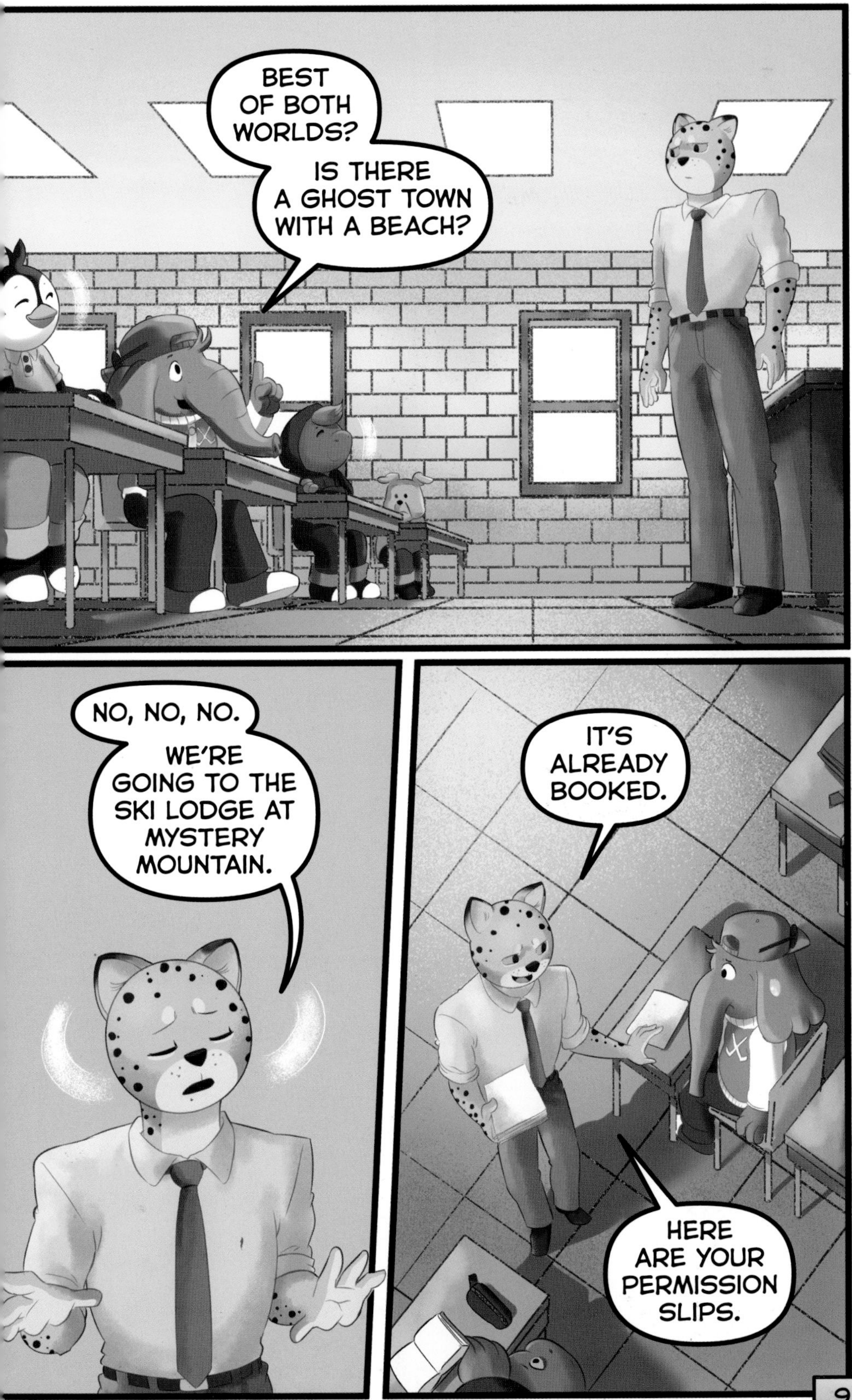
BEST OF BOTH WORLDS?
IS THERE A GHOST TOWN WITH A BEACH?
NO, NO, NO.
WE'RE GOING TO THE SKI LODGE AT MYSTERY MOUNTAIN.
IT'S ALREADY BOOKED.
HERE ARE YOUR PERMISSION SLIPS.

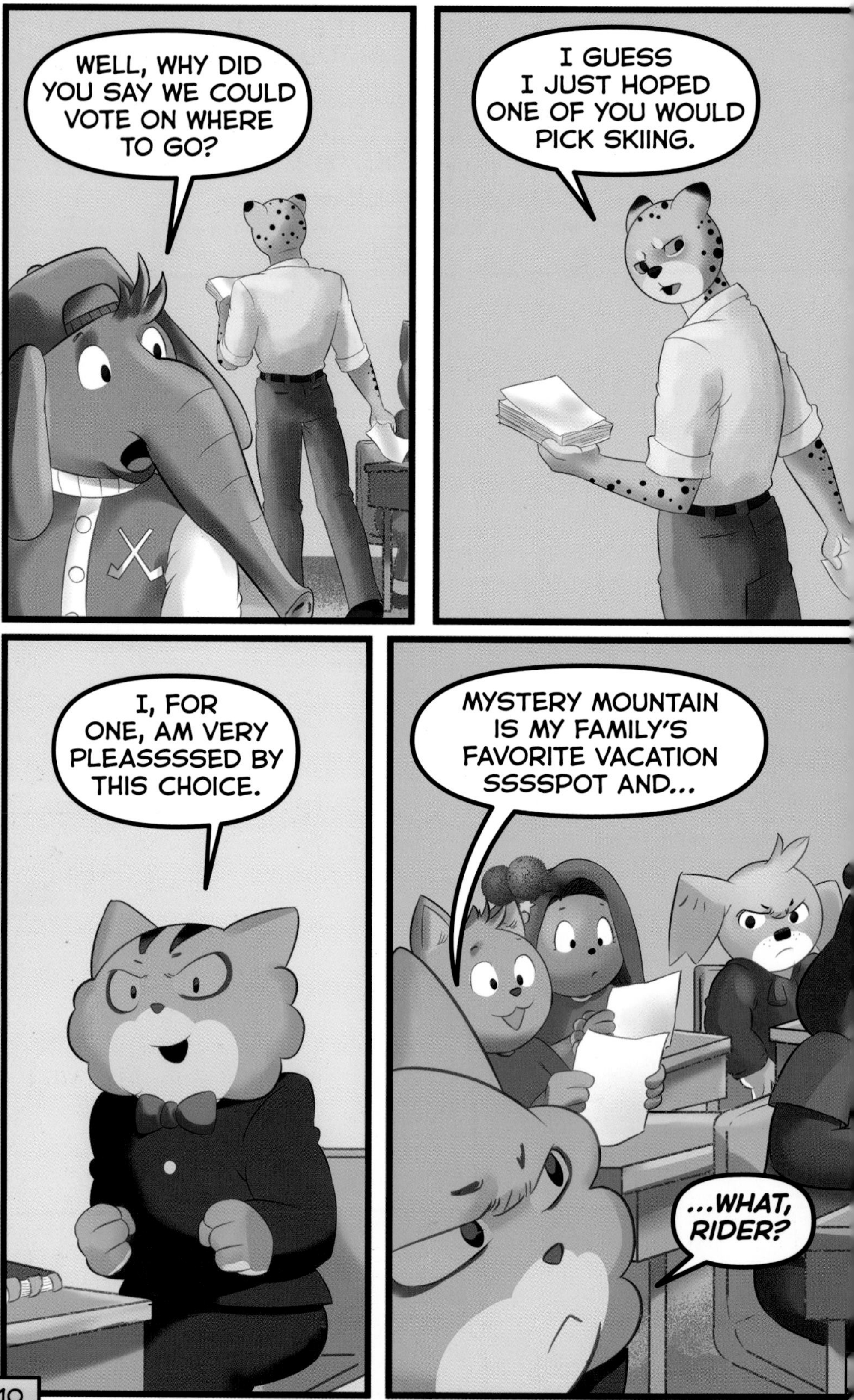
WELL, WHY DID YOU SAY WE COULD VOTE ON WHERE TO GO?
I GUESS I JUST HOPED ONE OF YOU WOULD PICK SKIING.
I, FOR ONE, AM VERY PLEASSSSED BY THIS CHOICE.
MYSTERY MOUNTAIN IS MY FAMILY'S FAVORITE VACATION SSSSPOT AND...
...WHAT, RIDER?

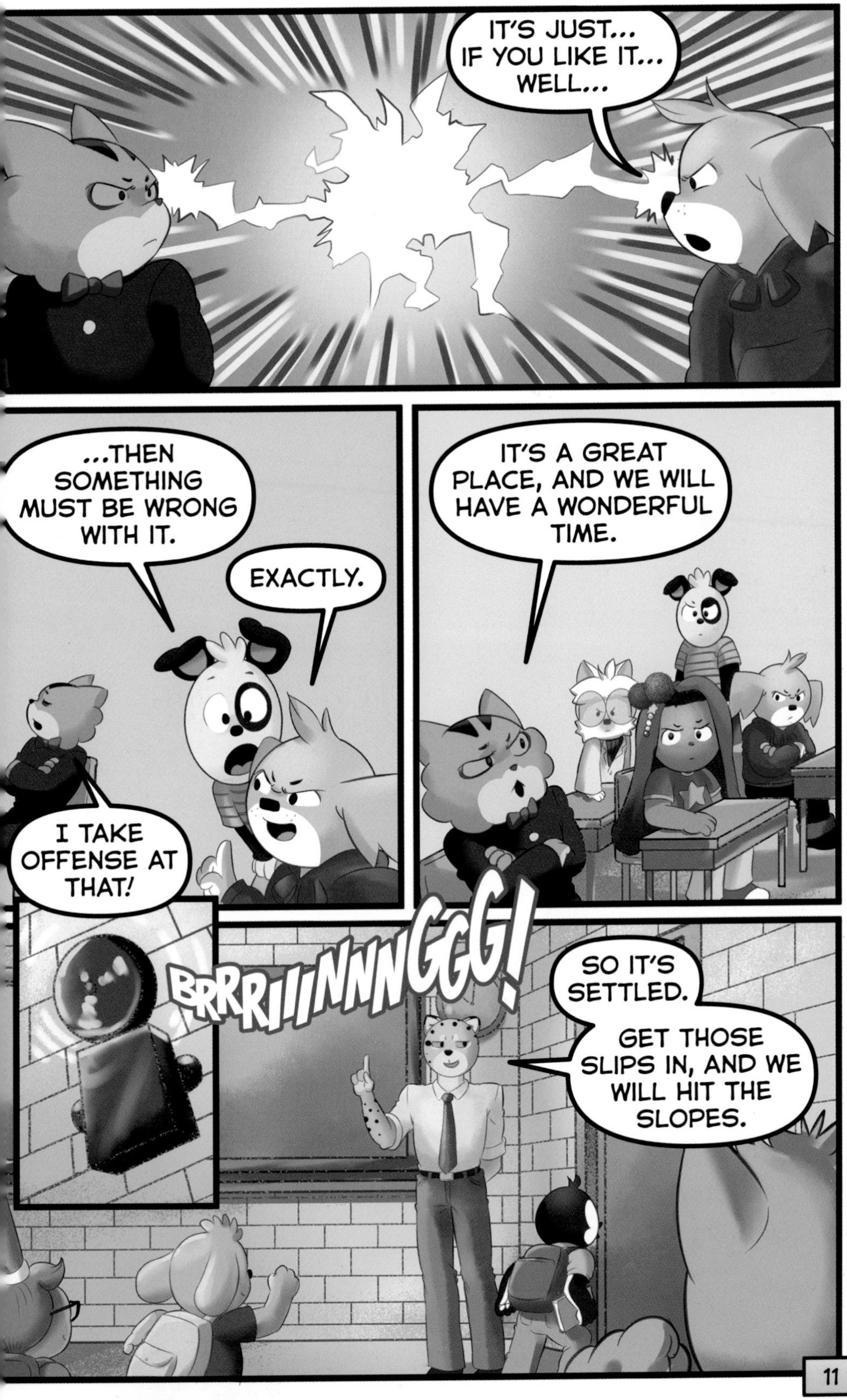
IT'S JUST... IF YOU LIKE IT... WELL...
...THEN SOMETHING MUST BE WRONG WITH IT.
EXACTLY.
I TAKE OFFENSE AT THAT!
IT'S A GREAT PLACE, AND WE WILL HAVE A WONDERFUL TIME.
BRRRIIINNNGGG!
SO IT'S SETTLED.
GET THOSE SLIPS IN, AND WE WILL HIT THE SLOPES.

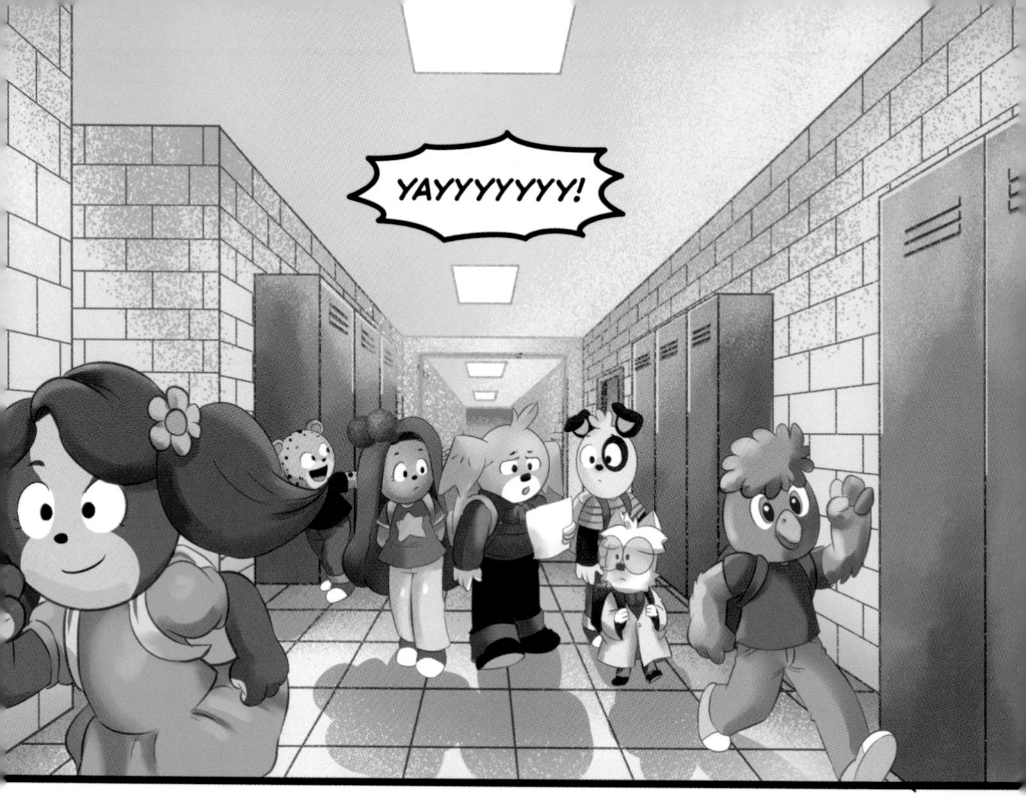
YAYYYYYYY!

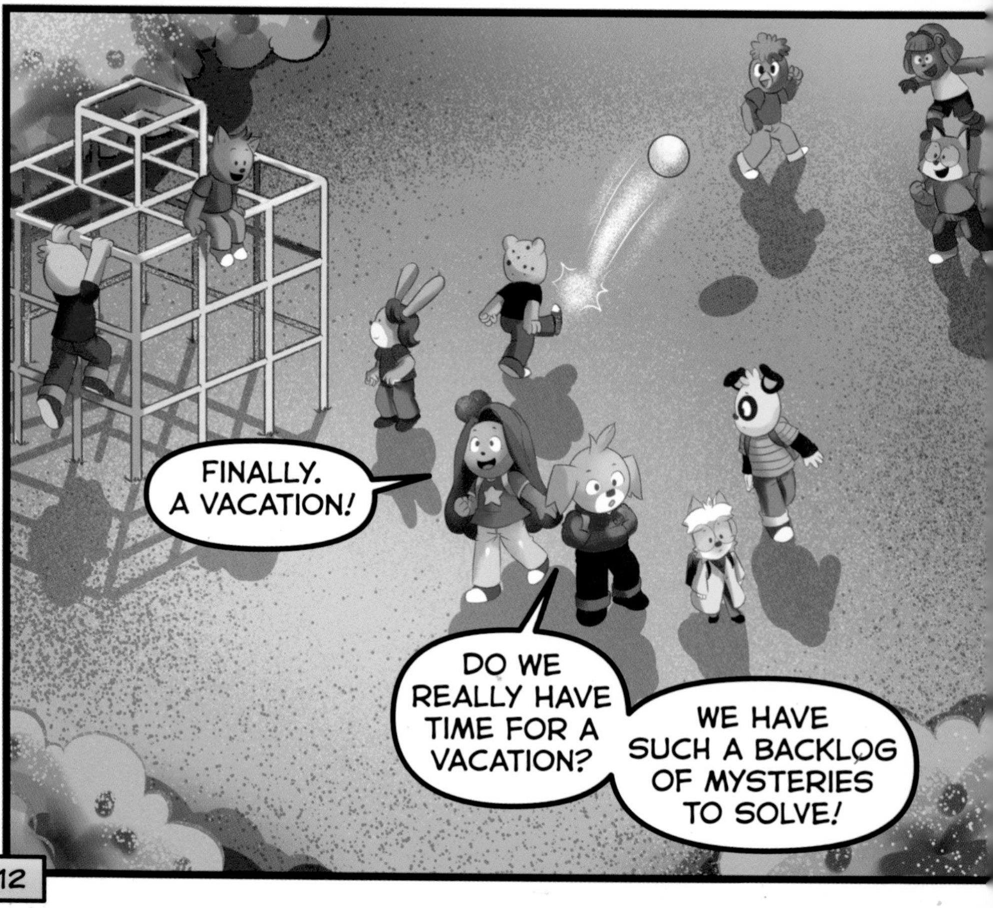
FINALLY. A VACATION!
DO WE REALLY HAVE TIME FOR A VACATION?
WE HAVE SUCH A BACKLOG OF MYSTERIES TO SOLVE!

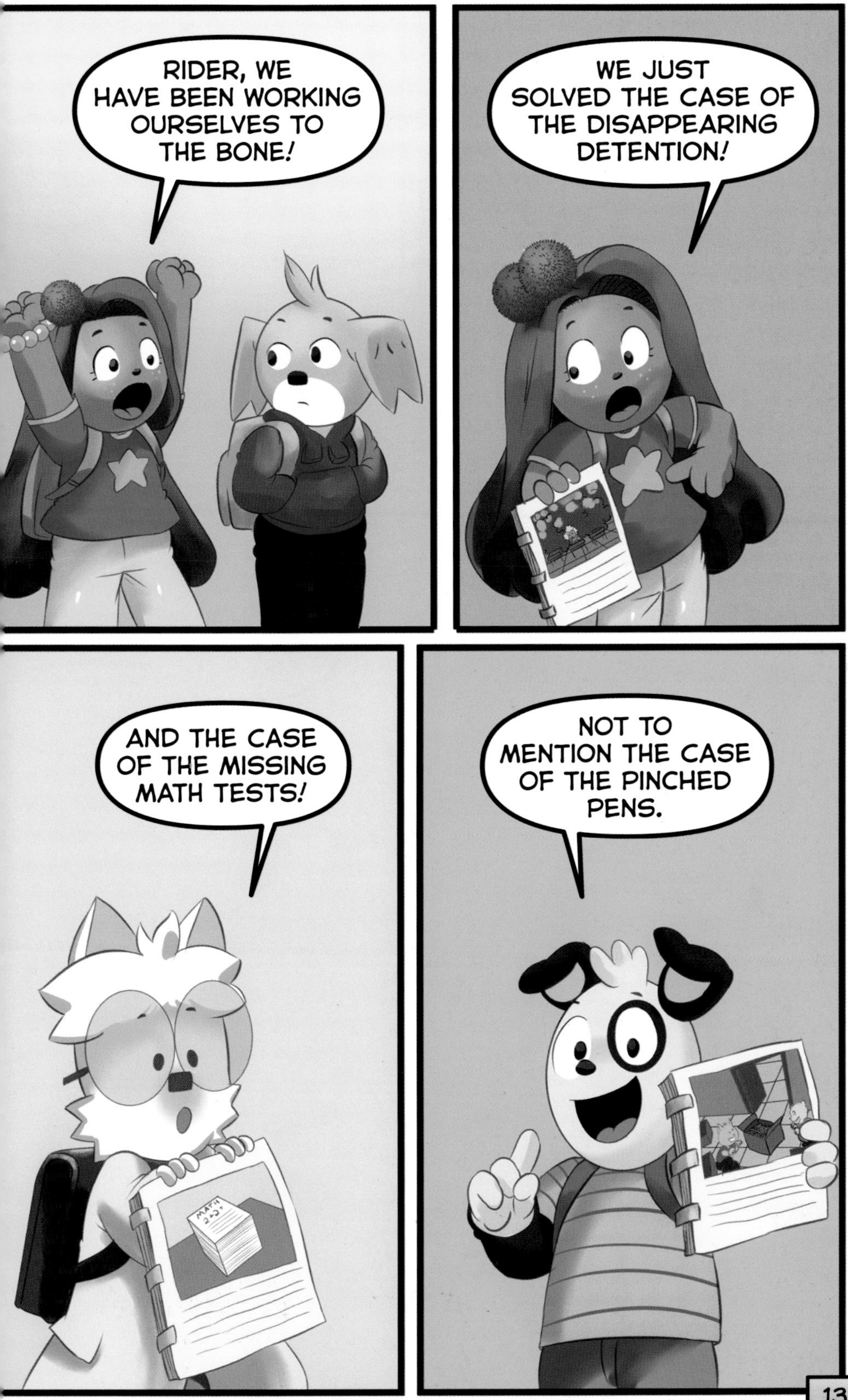
RIDER, WE HAVE BEEN WORKING OURSELVES TO THE BONE!
WE JUST SOLVED THE CASE OF THE DISAPPEARING DETENTION!
AND THE CASE OF THE MISSING MATH TESTS!
NOT TO MENTION THE CASE OF THE PINCHED PENS.

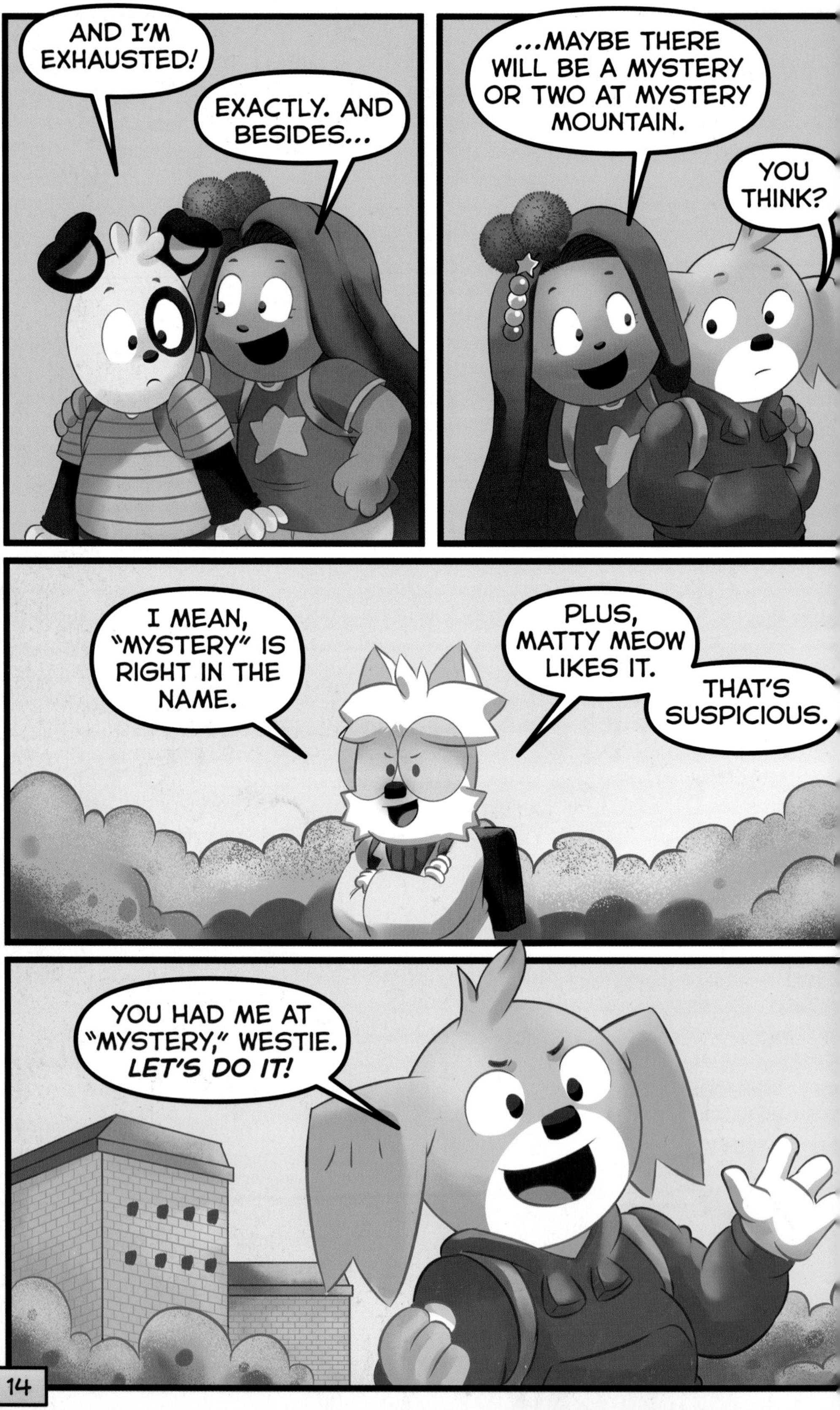
AND I'M EXHAUSTED!
EXACTLY. AND BESIDES...
...MAYBE THERE WILL BE A MYSTERY OR TWO AT MYSTERY MOUNTAIN.
YOU THINK?
I MEAN, "MYSTERY" IS RIGHT IN THE NAME.
PLUS, MATTY MEOW LIKES IT.
THAT'S SUSPICIOUS.
YOU HAD ME AT "MYSTERY," WESTIE. *LET'S DO IT!*

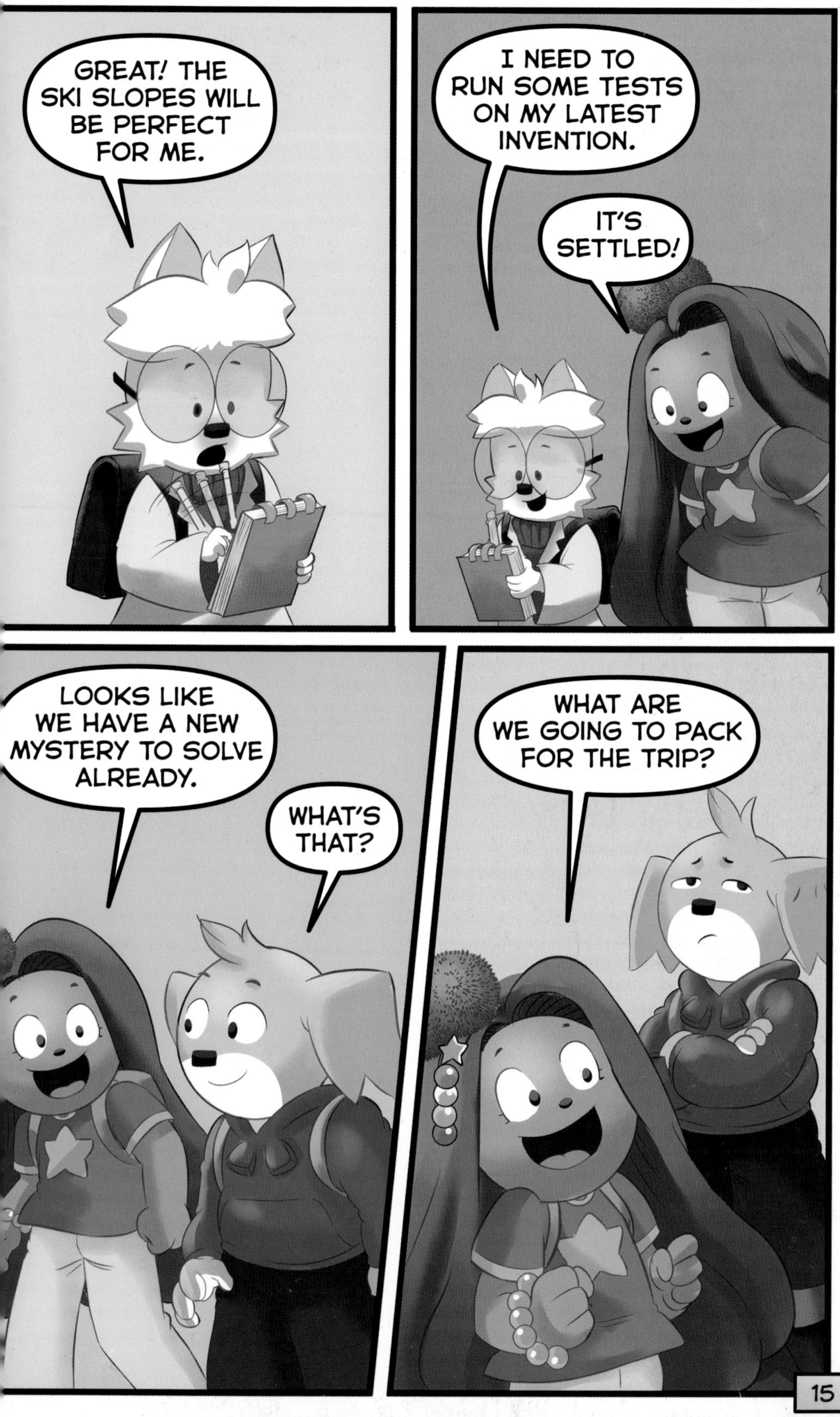
GREAT! THE SKI SLOPES WILL BE PERFECT FOR ME.
I NEED TO RUN SOME TESTS ON MY LATEST INVENTION.
IT'S SETTLED!
LOOKS LIKE WE HAVE A NEW MYSTERY TO SOLVE ALREADY.
WHAT'S THAT?
WHAT ARE WE GOING TO PACK FOR THE TRIP?

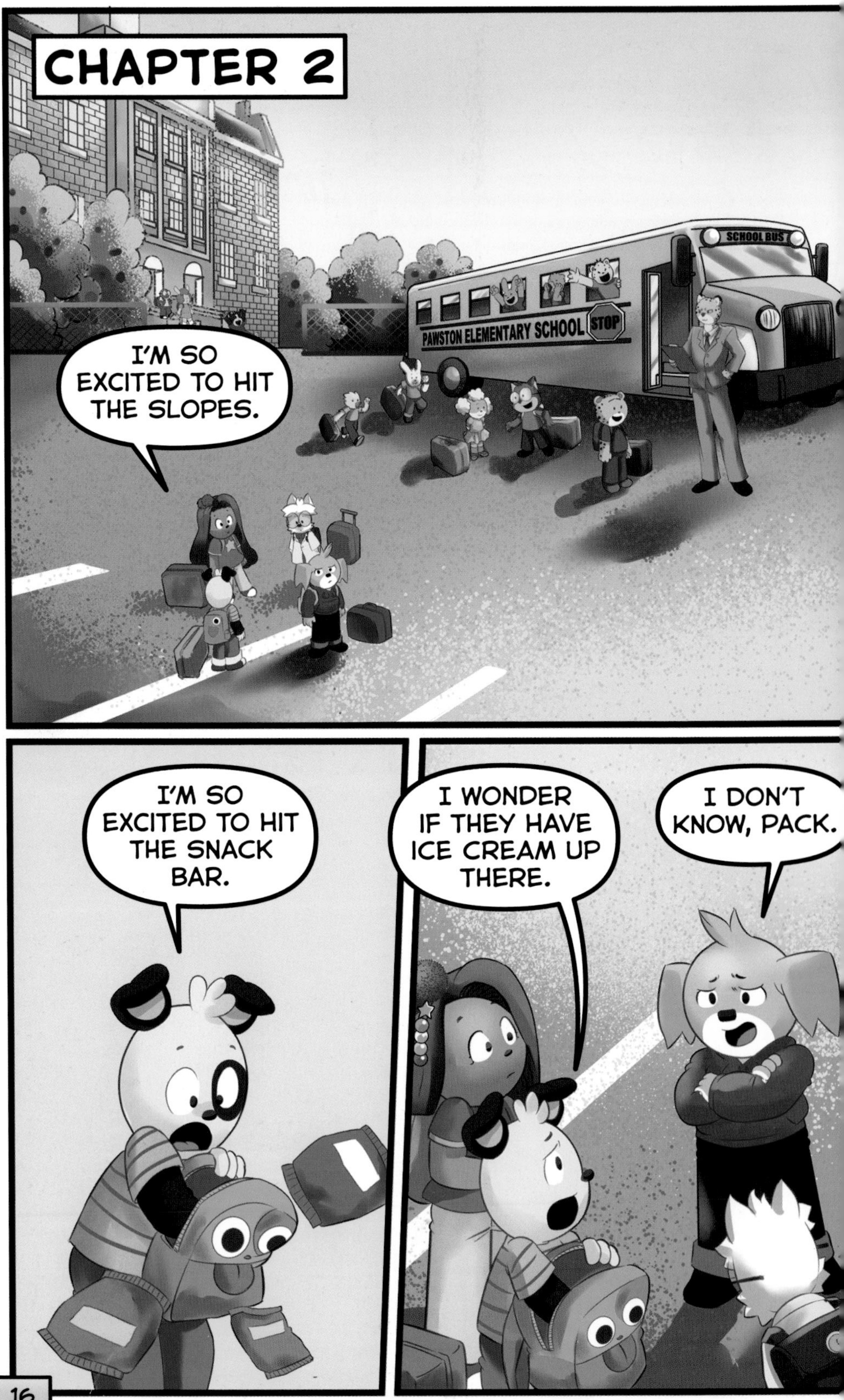
CHAPTER 2
SCHOOL BUS
PAWSTON ELEMENTARY SCHOOL
STOP
I'M SO EXCITED TO HIT THE SLOPES.
I'M SO EXCITED TO HIT THE SNACK BAR.
I WONDER IF THEY HAVE ICE CREAM UP THERE.
I DON'T KNOW, PACK.

IT STILL FEELS WRONG TO LEAVE ALL THE MYSTERIES AT SCHOOL BEHIND.

MAYBE I CAN AT LEAST GET SOME WORK DONE ON THE BUS.

ARE YOU BRINGING THOSE CASE FILES WITH YOU?

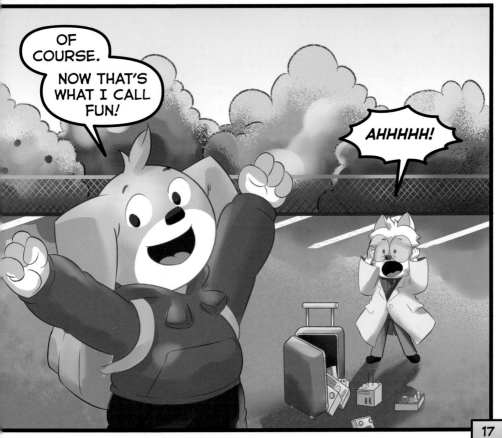

OF COURSE. NOW THAT'S WHAT I CALL FUN!

AHHHHH!

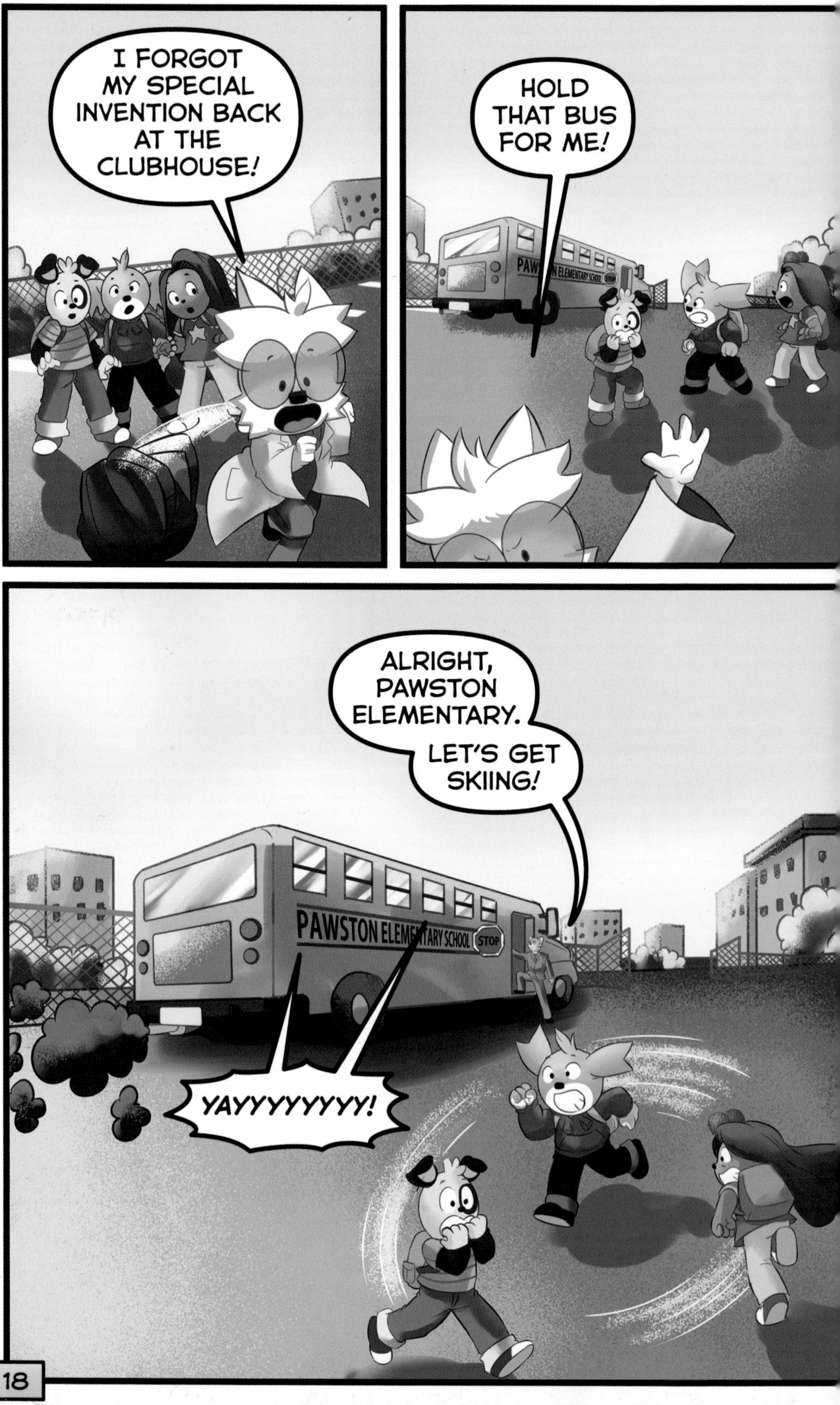
I FORGOT MY SPECIAL INVENTION BACK AT THE CLUBHOUSE!
HOLD THAT BUS FOR ME!
ALRIGHT, PAWSTON ELEMENTARY.
LET'S GET SKIING!
PAWSTON ELEMENTARY SCHOOL
STOP
YAYYYYYYYYY!

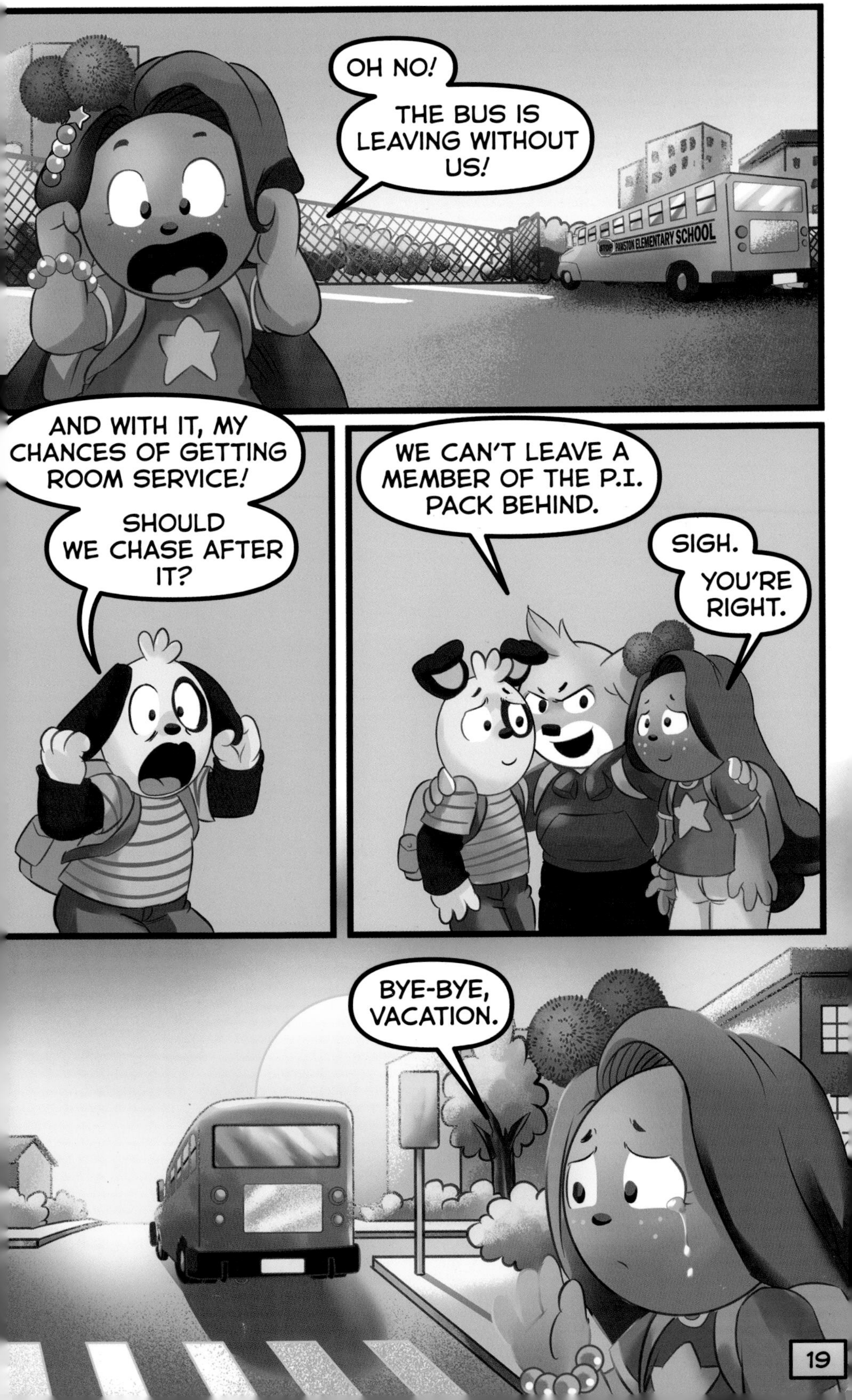
OH NO!
THE BUS IS LEAVING WITHOUT US!
PAWSTON ELEMENTARY SCHOOL
AND WITH IT, MY CHANCES OF GETTING ROOM SERVICE!
SHOULD WE CHASE AFTER IT?
WE CAN'T LEAVE A MEMBER OF THE P.I. PACK BEHIND.
SIGH.
YOU'RE RIGHT.
BYE-BYE, VACATION.

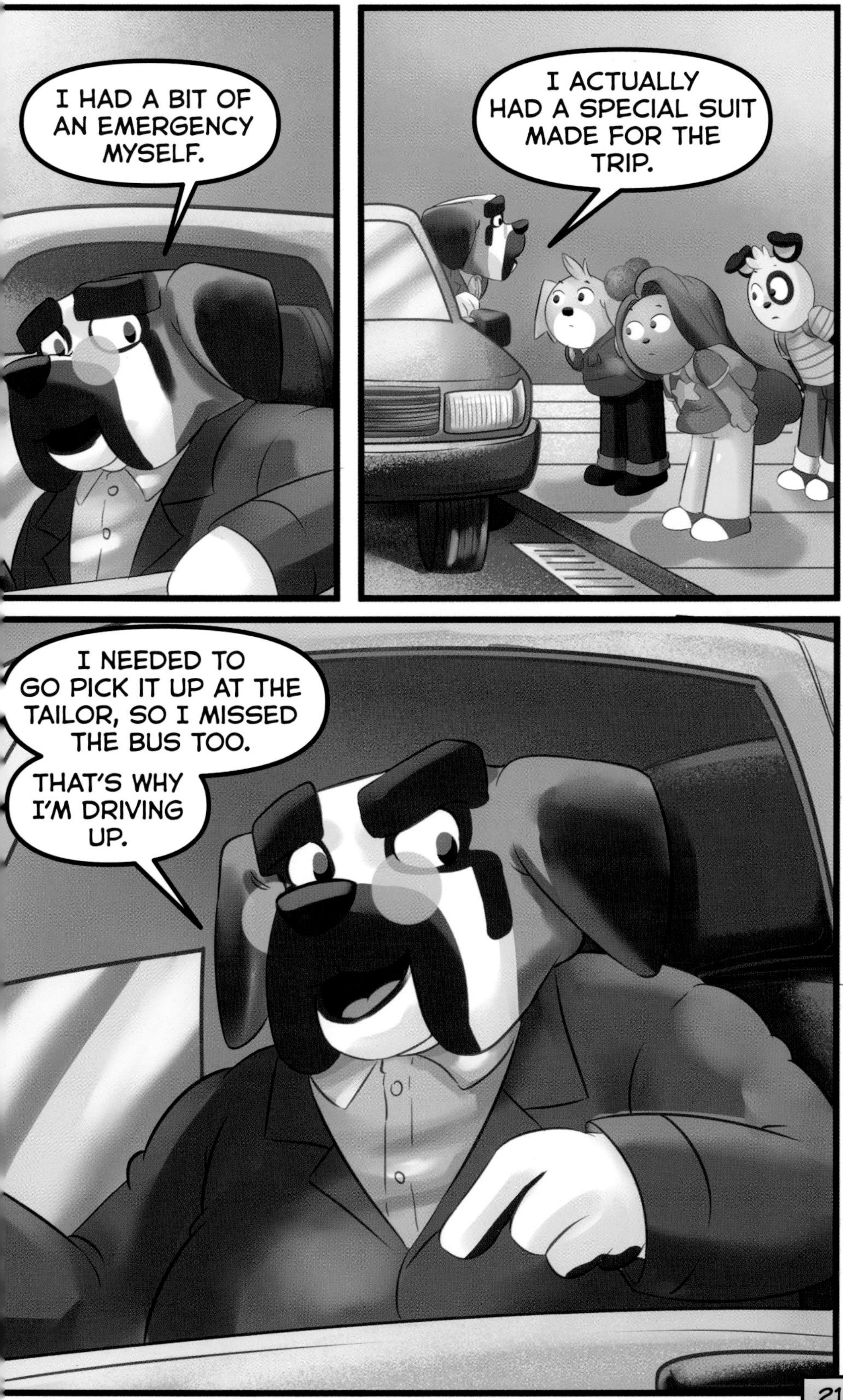
I HAD A BIT OF AN EMERGENCY MYSELF.
I ACTUALLY HAD A SPECIAL SUIT MADE FOR THE TRIP.
I NEEDED TO GO PICK IT UP AT THE TAILOR, SO I MISSED THE BUS TOO.
THAT'S WHY I'M DRIVING UP.

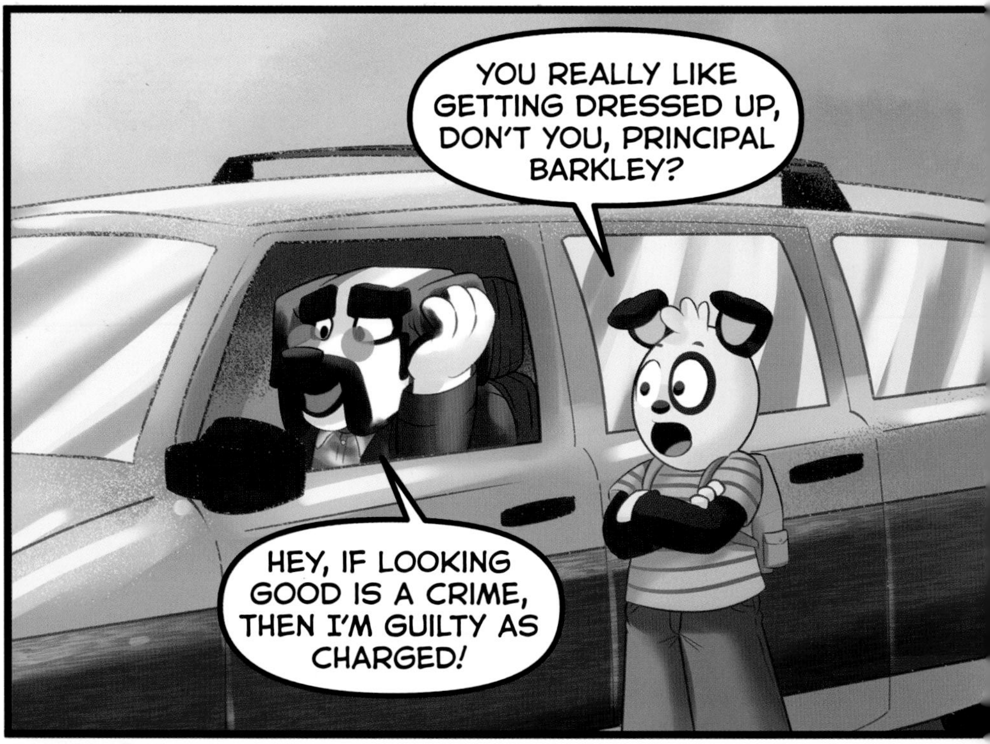
YOU REALLY LIKE GETTING DRESSED UP, DON'T YOU, PRINCIPAL BARKLEY?
HEY, IF LOOKING GOOD IS A CRIME, THEN I'M GUILTY AS CHARGED!

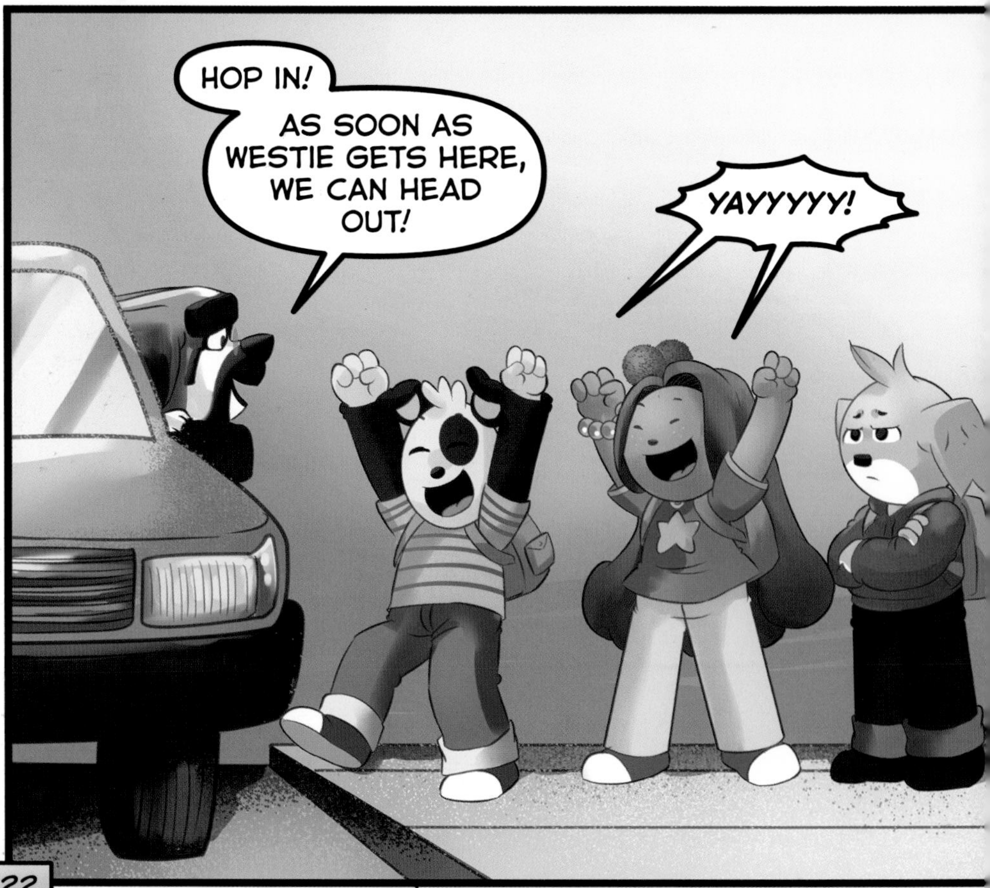
HOP IN!
AS SOON AS WESTIE GETS HERE, WE CAN HEAD OUT!
YAYYYYY!

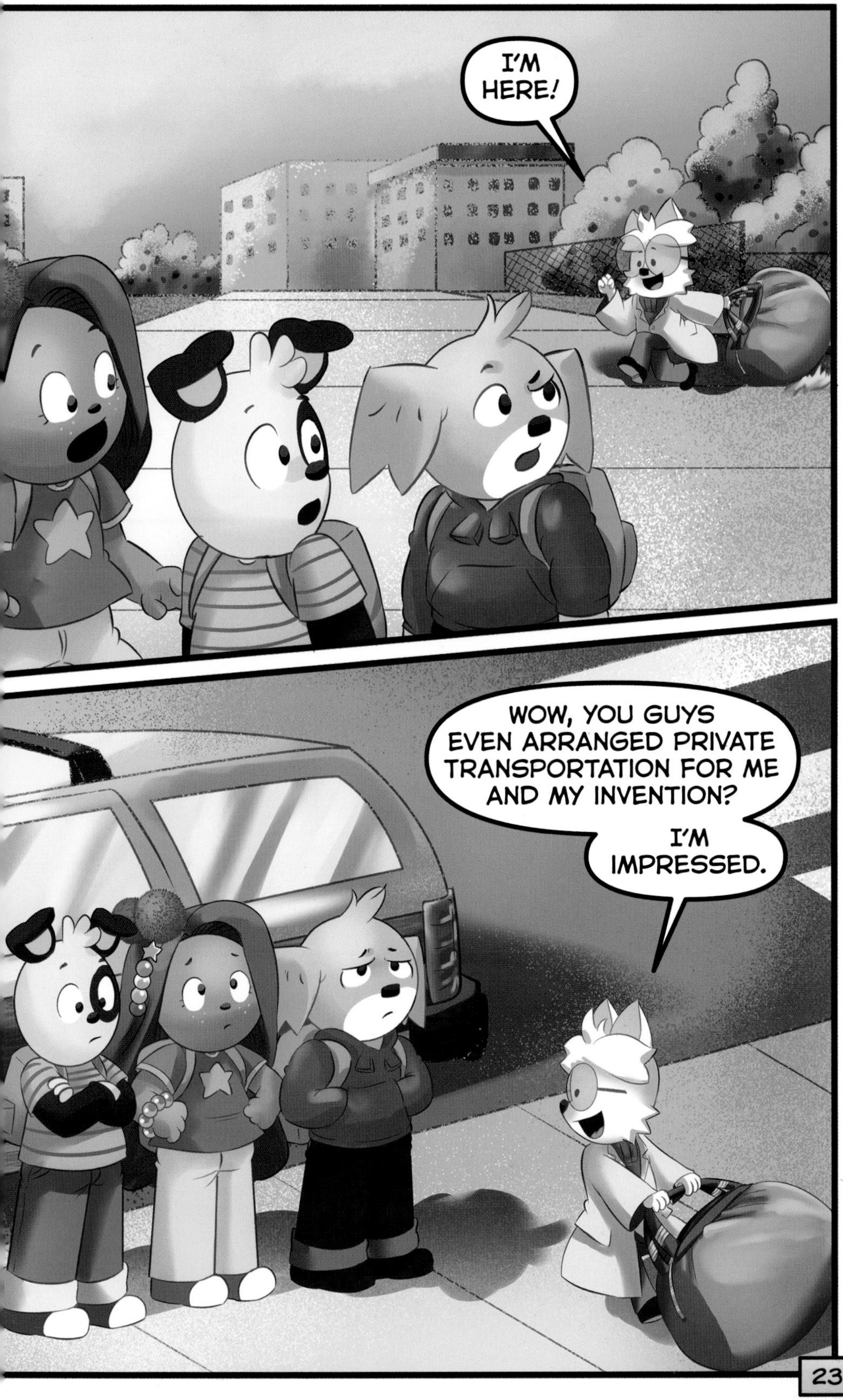
I'M HERE!
WOW, YOU GUYS EVEN ARRANGED PRIVATE TRANSPORTATION FOR ME AND MY INVENTION?
I'M IMPRESSED.

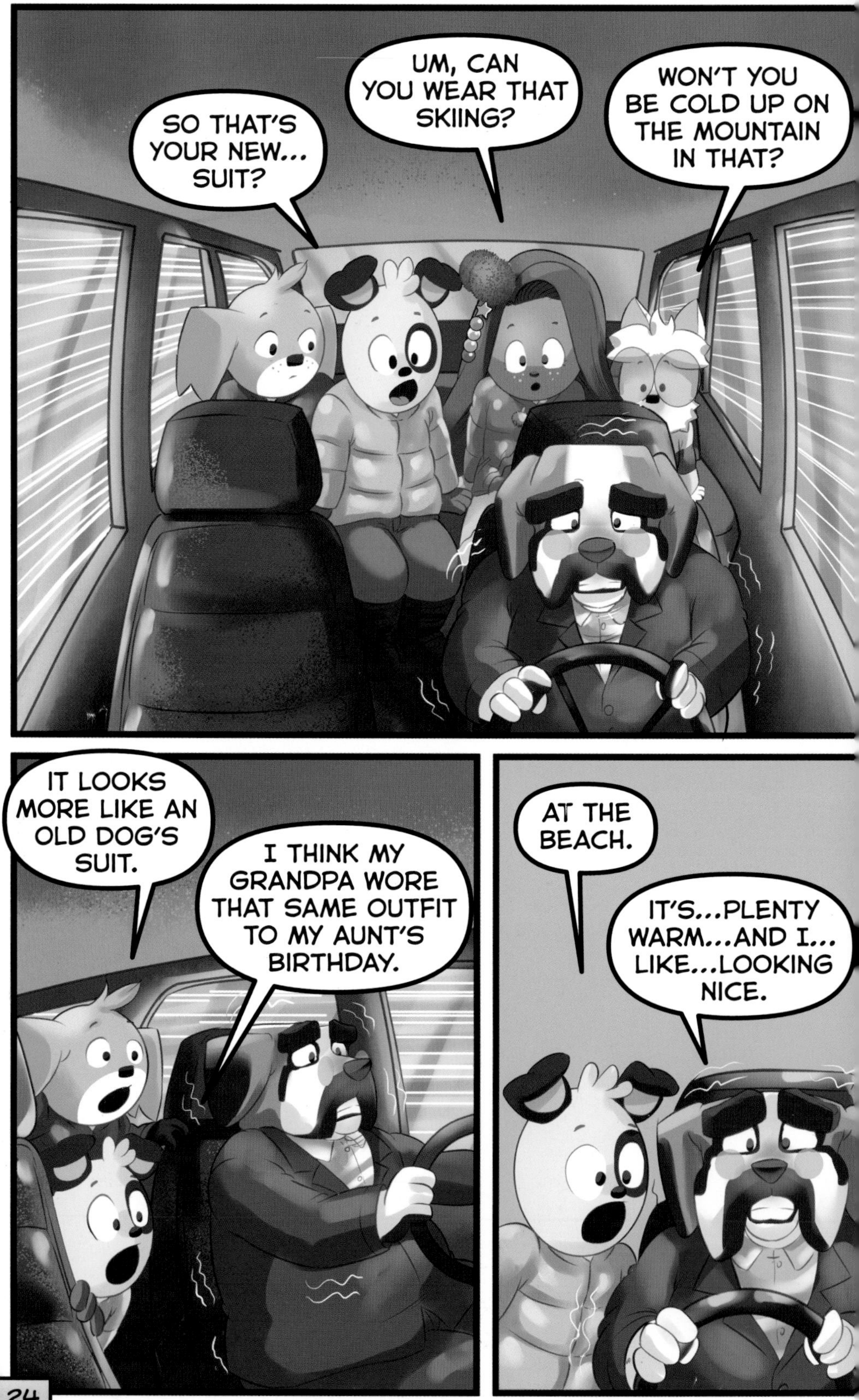
SO THAT'S YOUR NEW... SUIT?
UM, CAN YOU WEAR THAT SKIING?
WON'T YOU BE COLD UP ON THE MOUNTAIN IN THAT?
IT LOOKS MORE LIKE AN OLD DOG'S SUIT.
I THINK MY GRANDPA WORE THAT SAME OUTFIT TO MY AUNT'S BIRTHDAY.
AT THE BEACH.
IT'S...PLENTY WARM...AND I... LIKE...LOOKING NICE.

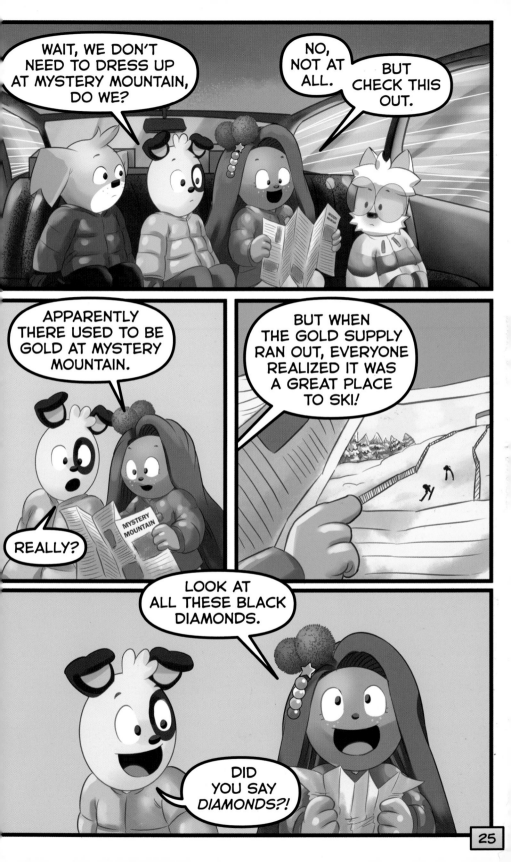

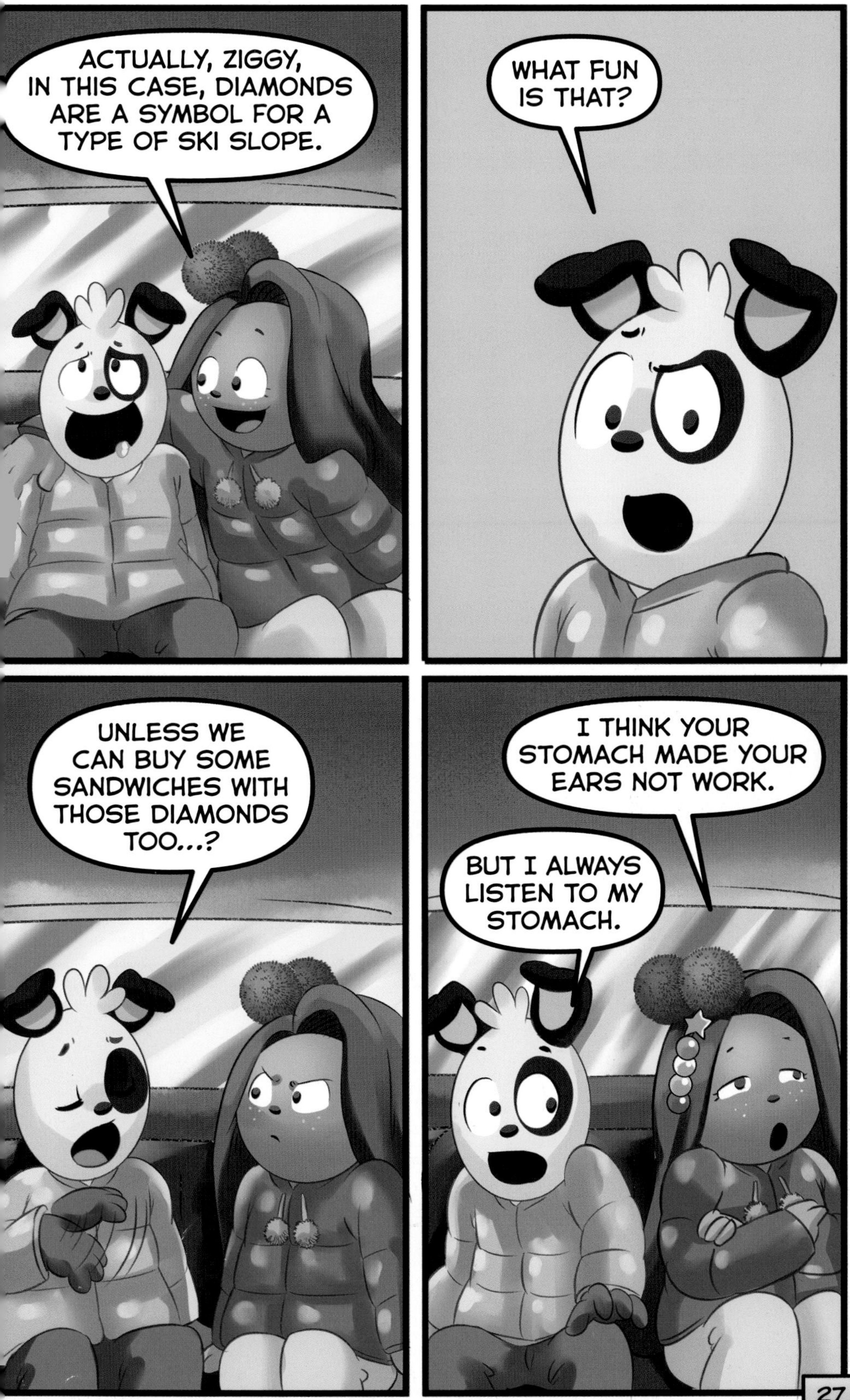
ACTUALLY, ZIGGY, IN THIS CASE, DIAMONDS ARE A SYMBOL FOR A TYPE OF SKI SLOPE.
WHAT FUN IS THAT?
UNLESS WE CAN BUY SOME SANDWICHES WITH THOSE DIAMONDS TOO...?
I THINK YOUR STOMACH MADE YOUR EARS NOT WORK.
BUT I ALWAYS LISTEN TO MY STOMACH.

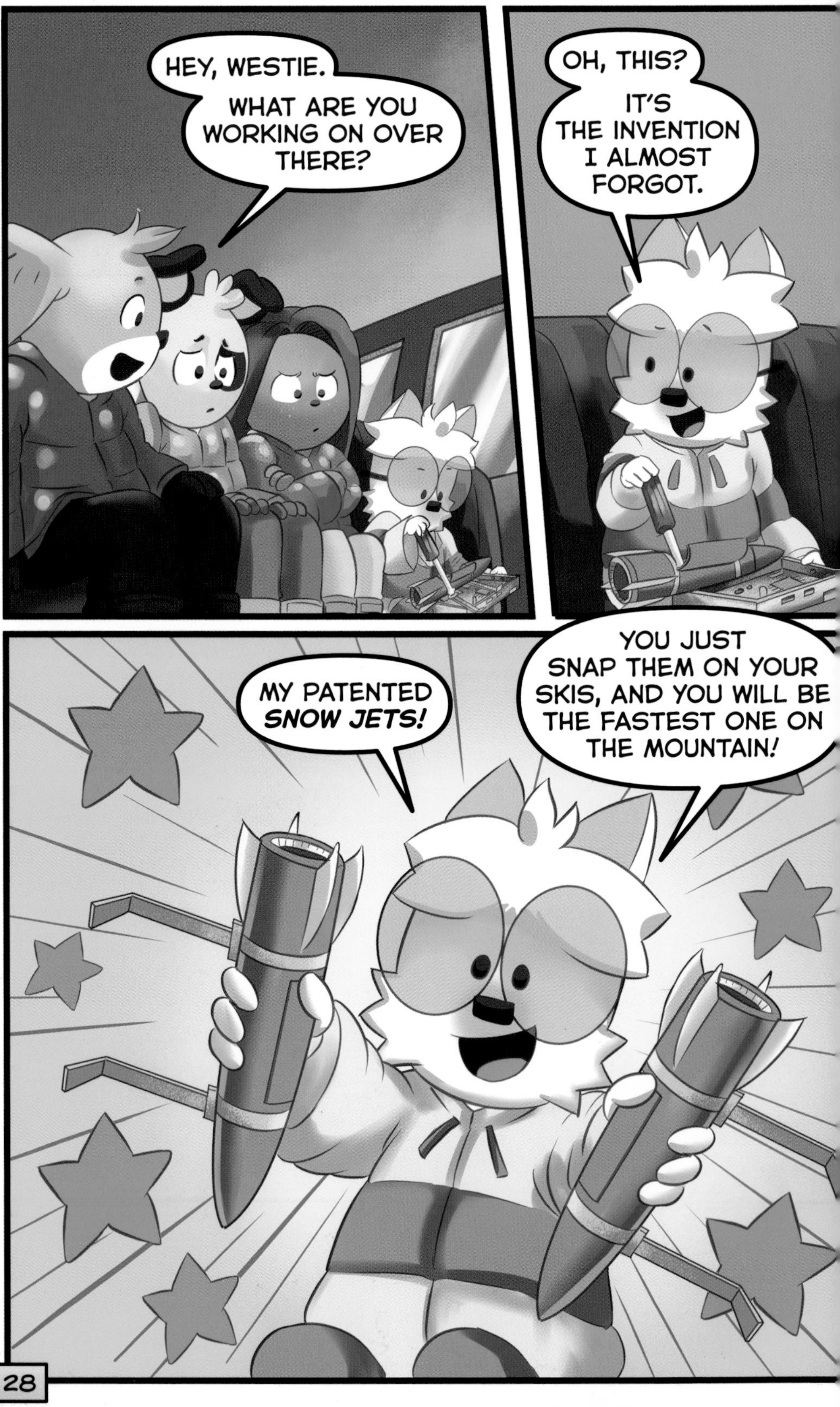
HEY, WESTIE.
WHAT ARE YOU WORKING ON OVER THERE?
OH, THIS?
IT'S THE INVENTION I ALMOST FORGOT.
MY PATENTED *SNOW JETS!*
YOU JUST SNAP THEM ON YOUR SKIS, AND YOU WILL BE THE FASTEST ONE ON THE MOUNTAIN!

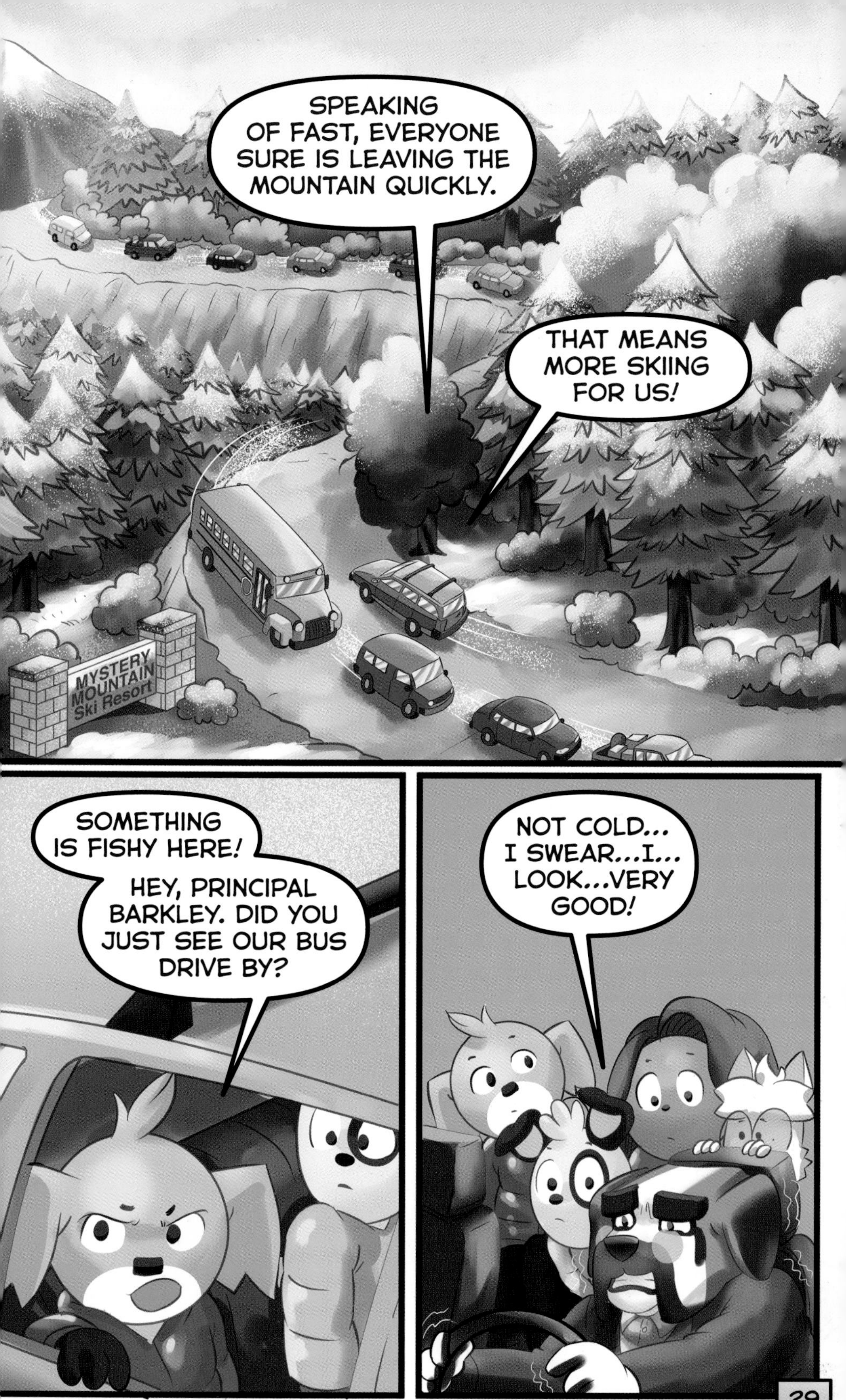
SPEAKING OF FAST, EVERYONE SURE IS LEAVING THE MOUNTAIN QUICKLY.
THAT MEANS MORE SKIING FOR US!
MYSTERY MOUNTAIN Ski Resort
SOMETHING IS FISHY HERE!
HEY, PRINCIPAL BARKLEY. DID YOU JUST SEE OUR BUS DRIVE BY?
NOT COLD... I SWEAR...I... LOOK...VERY GOOD!

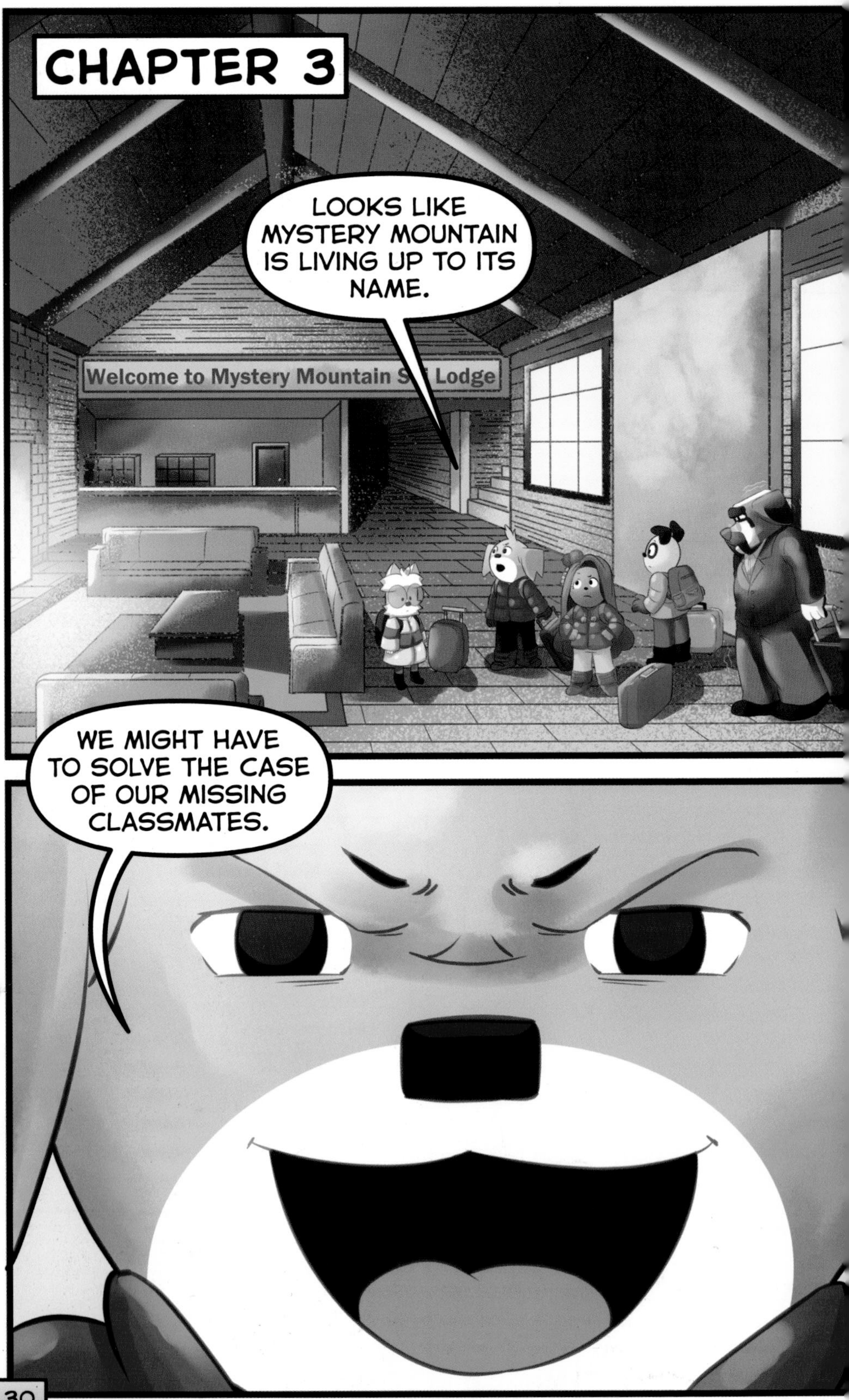
CHAPTER 3
LOOKS LIKE MYSTERY MOUNTAIN IS LIVING UP TO ITS NAME.
Welcome to Mystery Mountain S Lodge
WE MIGHT HAVE TO SOLVE THE CASE OF OUR MISSING CLASSMATES.

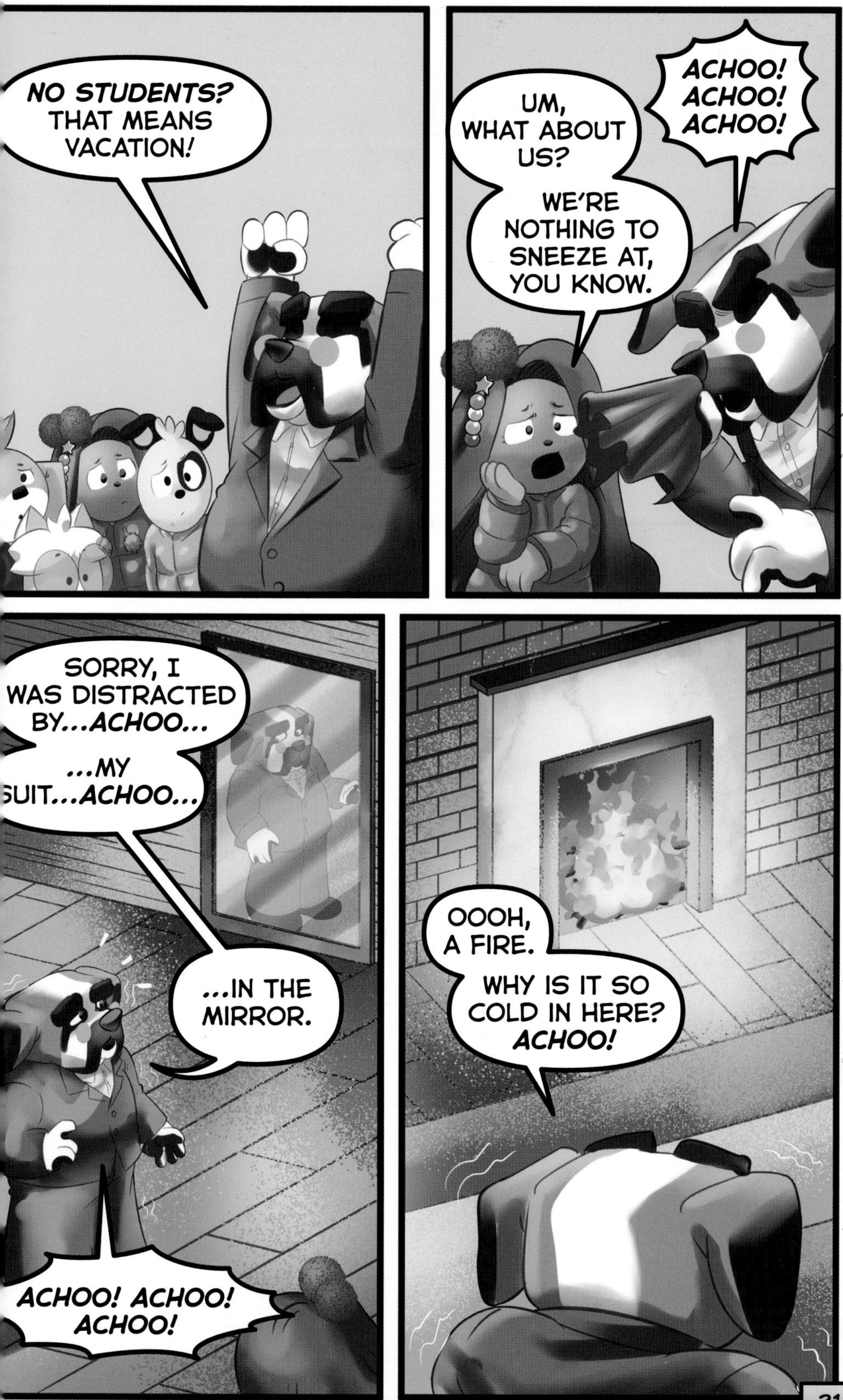

NO STUDENTS? THAT MEANS VACATION!
UM, WHAT ABOUT US?
WE'RE NOTHING TO SNEEZE AT, YOU KNOW.
ACHOO! ACHOO! ACHOO!
SORRY, I WAS DISTRACTED BY...ACHOO...
...MY SUIT...ACHOO...
...IN THE MIRROR.
ACHOO! ACHOO! ACHOO!
OOOH, A FIRE.
WHY IS IT SO COLD IN HERE? ACHOO!

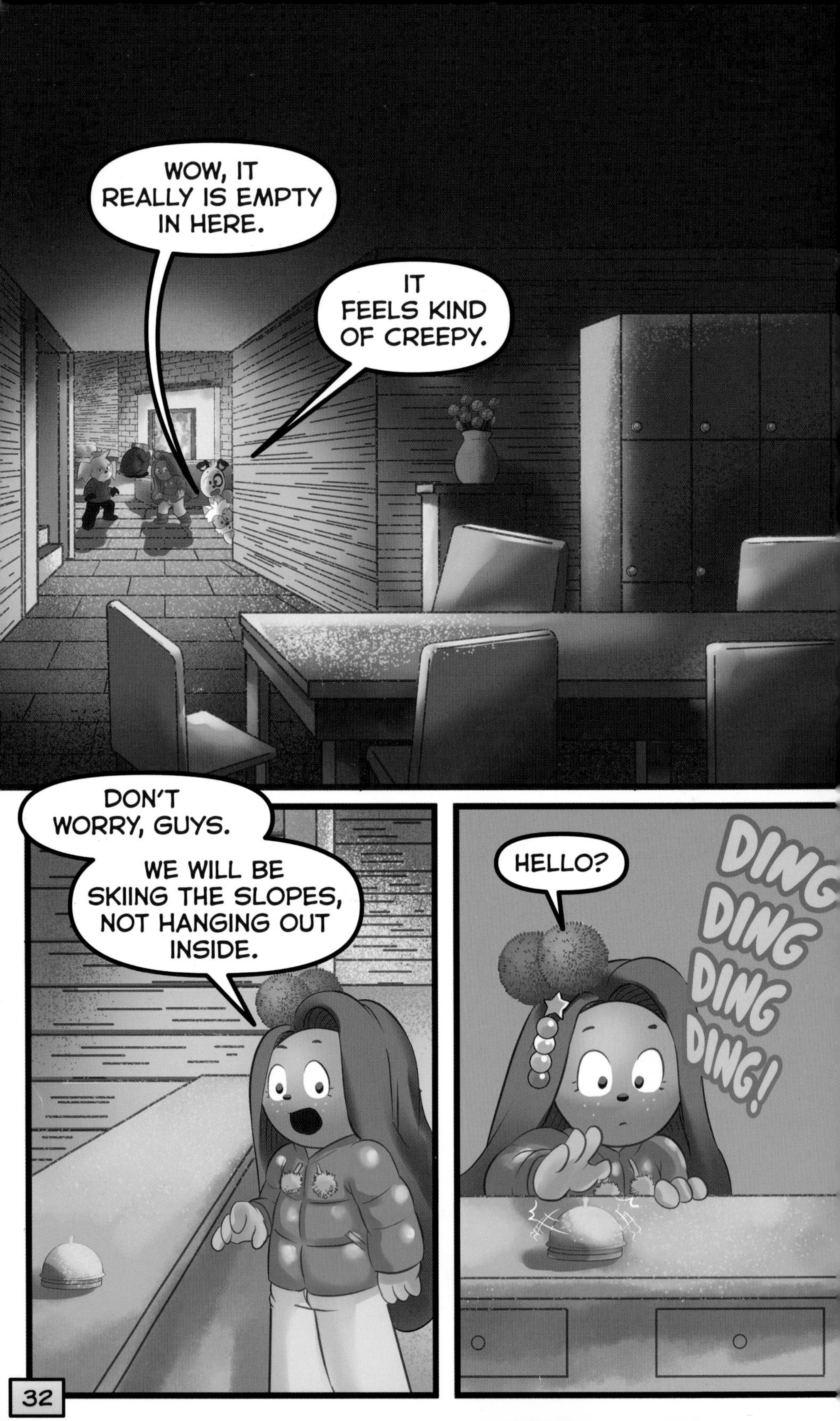
WOW, IT REALLY IS EMPTY IN HERE.
IT FEELS KIND OF CREEPY.
DON'T WORRY, GUYS.
WE WILL BE SKIING THE SLOPES, NOT HANGING OUT INSIDE.
HELLO?
DING DING DING DING!

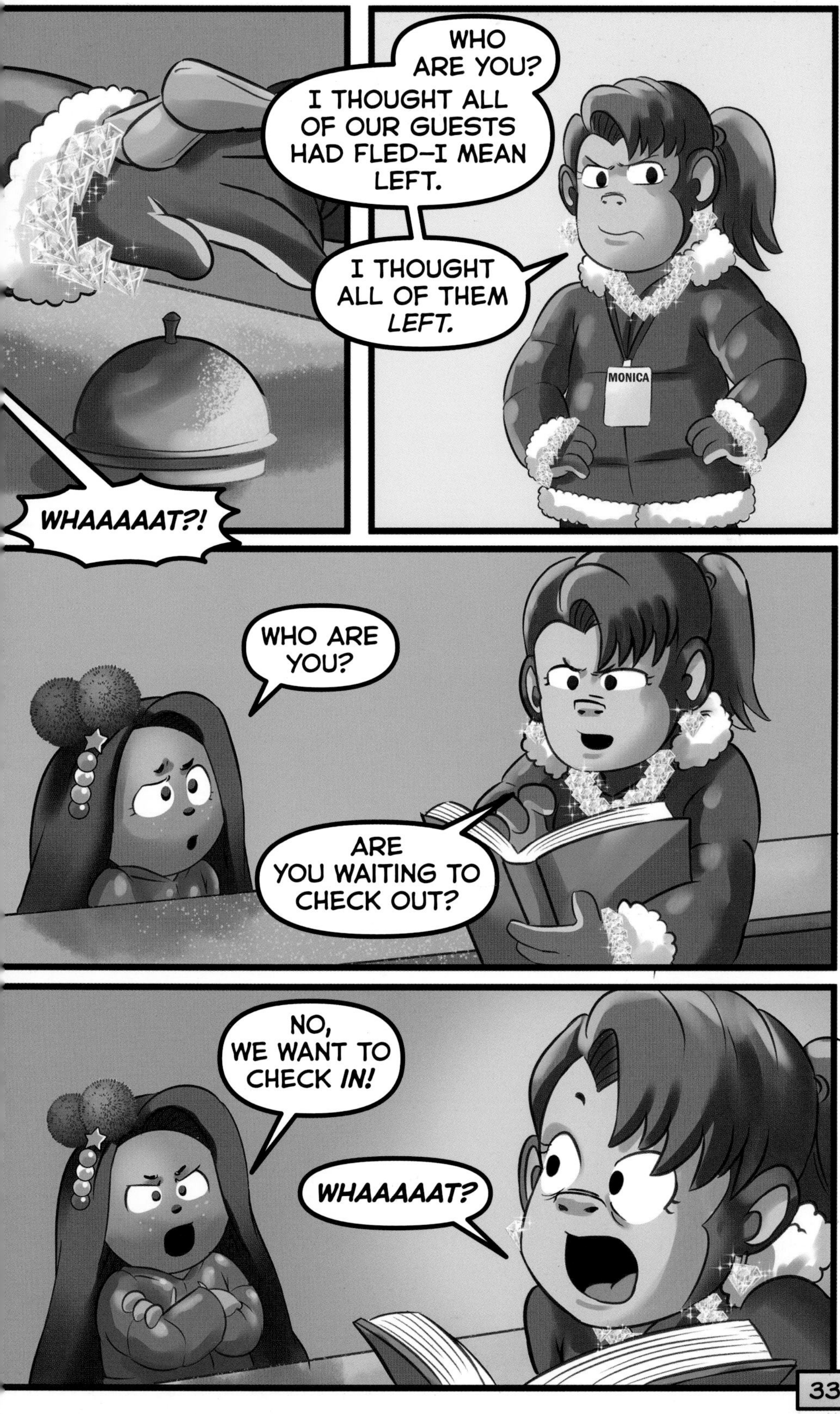
WHO ARE YOU?
I THOUGHT ALL OF OUR GUESTS HAD FLED—I MEAN LEFT.
I THOUGHT ALL OF THEM *LEFT.*
MONICA
WHAAAAAT?!
WHO ARE YOU?
ARE YOU WAITING TO CHECK OUT?
NO, WE WANT TO CHECK *IN!*
WHAAAAAT?

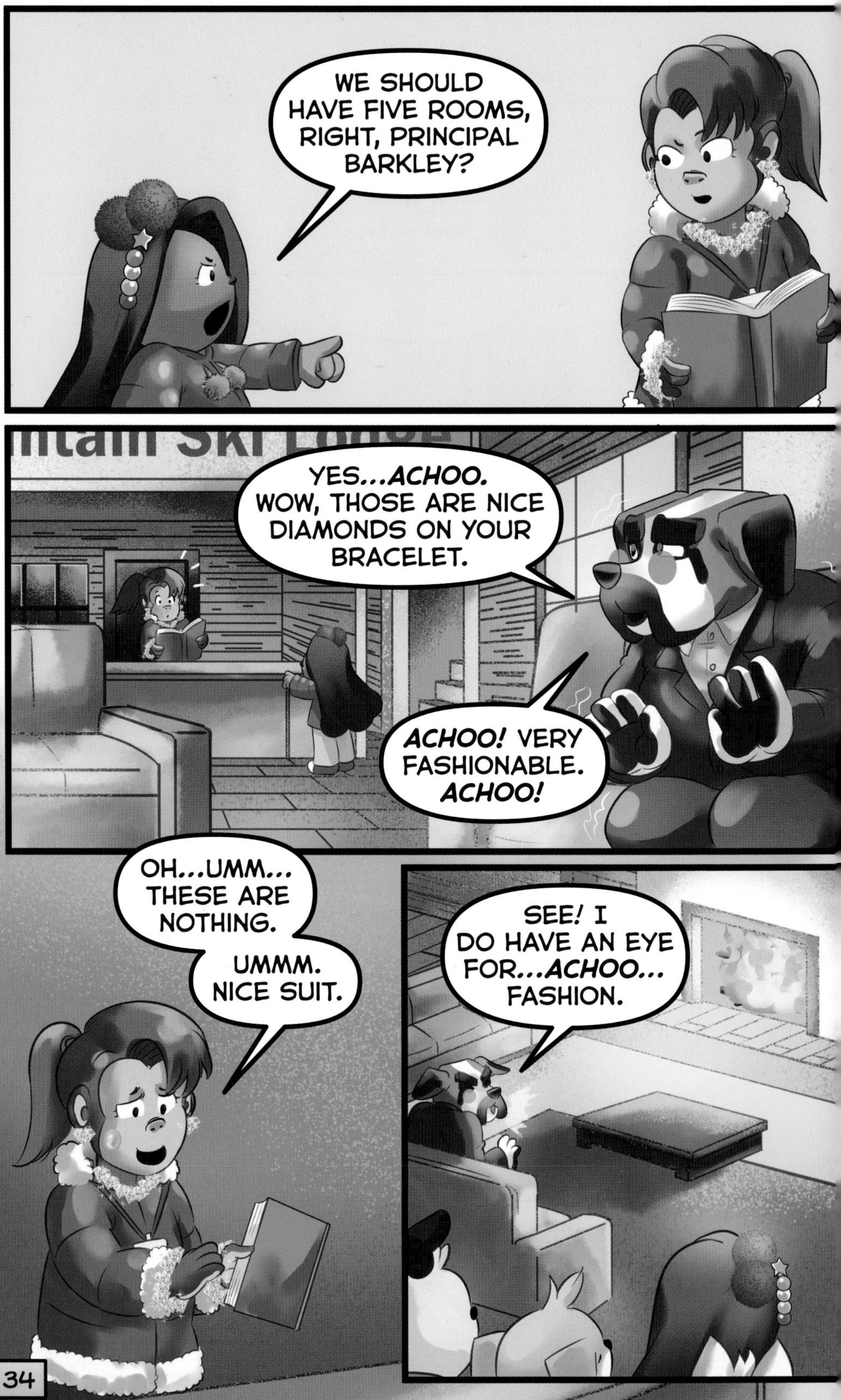
WE SHOULD HAVE FIVE ROOMS, RIGHT, PRINCIPAL BARKLEY?
YES...ACHOO. WOW, THOSE ARE NICE DIAMONDS ON YOUR BRACELET.
ACHOO! VERY FASHIONABLE. ACHOO!
OH...UMM... THESE ARE NOTHING.
UMMM. NICE SUIT.
SEE! I DO HAVE AN EYE FOR...ACHOO... FASHION.

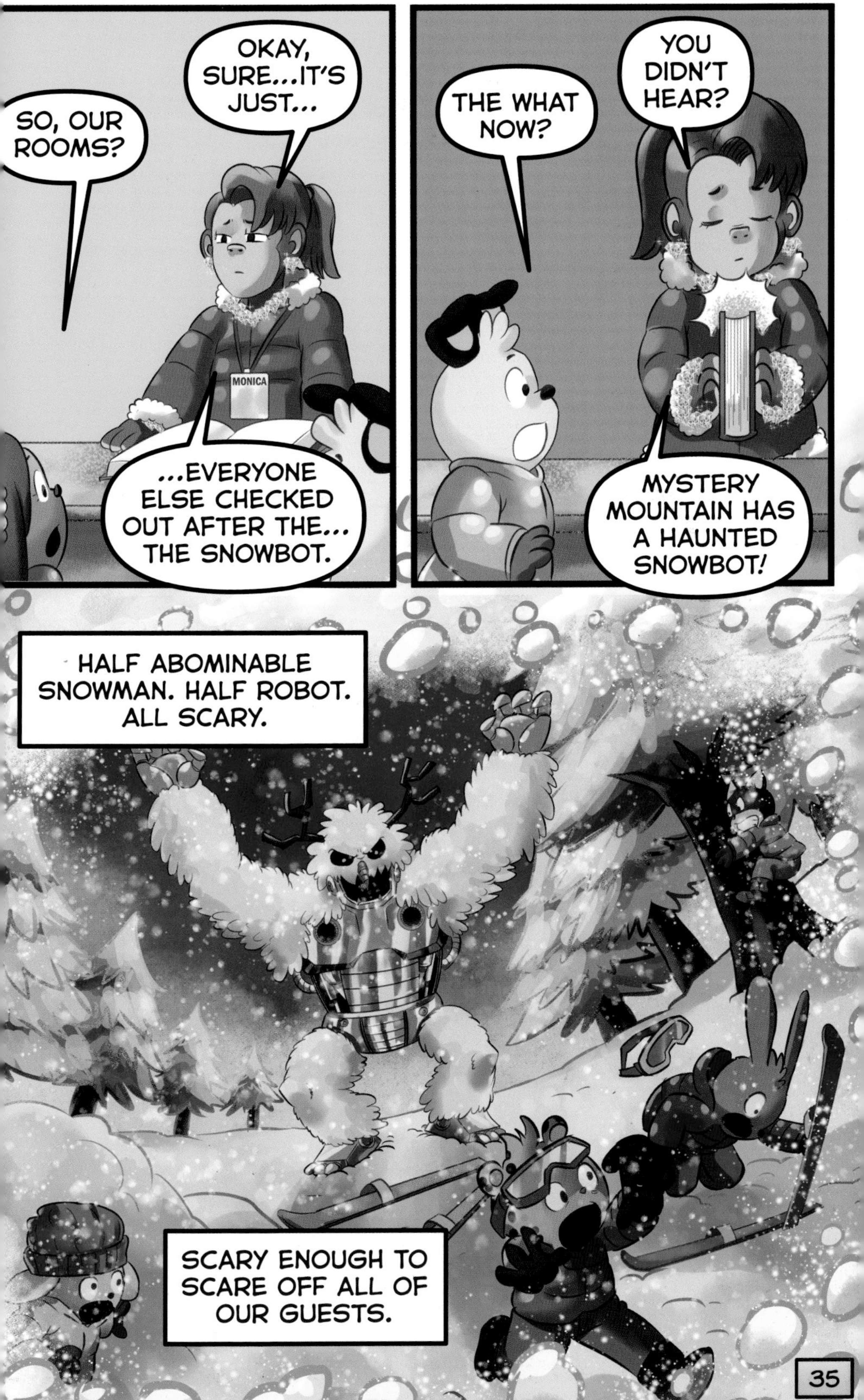
SO, OUR ROOMS?
OKAY, SURE...IT'S JUST...
MONICA
...EVERYONE ELSE CHECKED OUT AFTER THE... THE SNOWBOT.
THE WHAT NOW?
YOU DIDN'T HEAR?
MYSTERY MOUNTAIN HAS A HAUNTED SNOWBOT!
HALF ABOMINABLE SNOWMAN. HALF ROBOT. ALL SCARY.
SCARY ENOUGH TO SCARE OFF ALL OF OUR GUESTS.

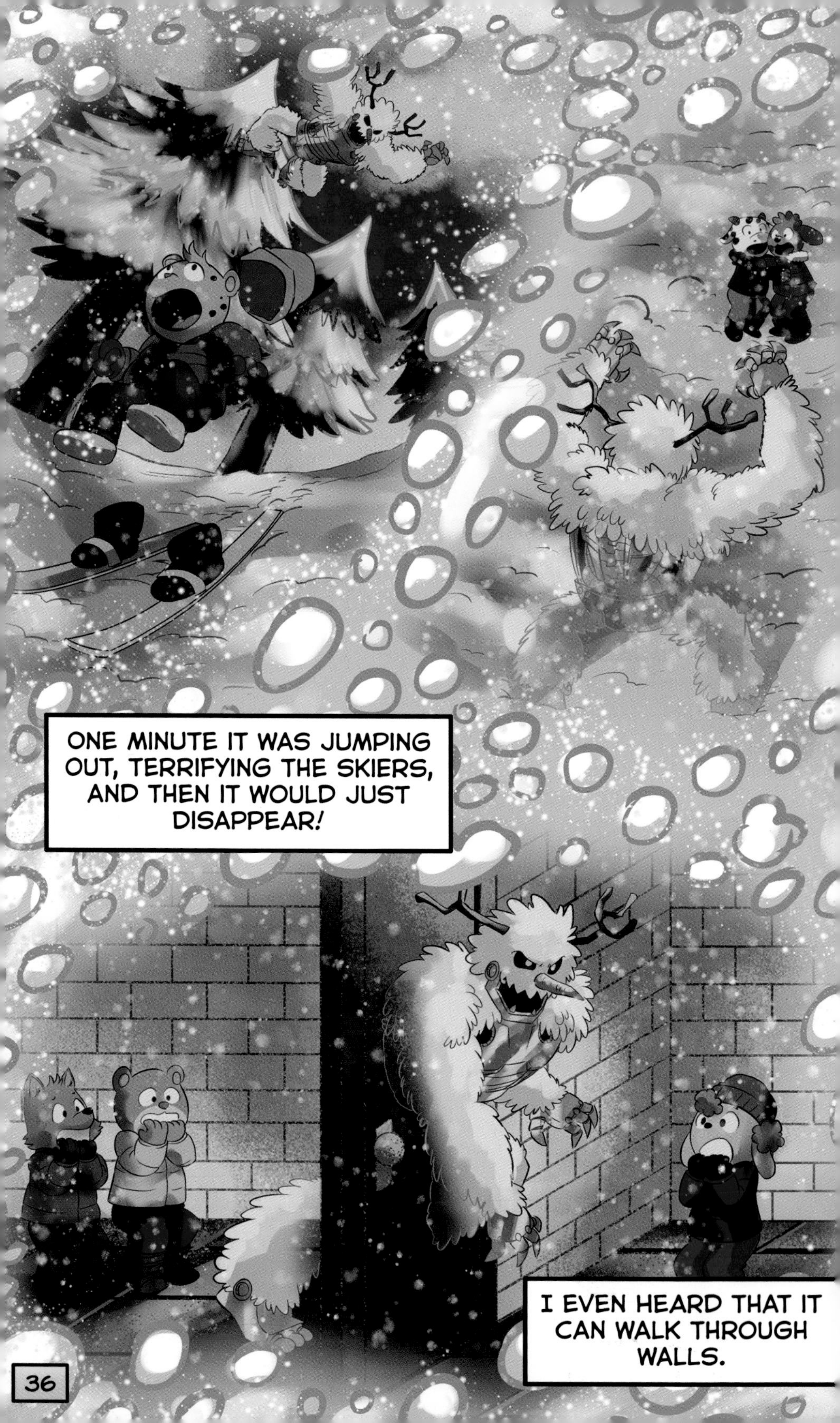
ONE MINUTE IT WAS JUMPING OUT, TERRIFYING THE SKIERS, AND THEN IT WOULD JUST DISAPPEAR!
I EVEN HEARD THAT IT CAN WALK THROUGH WALLS.

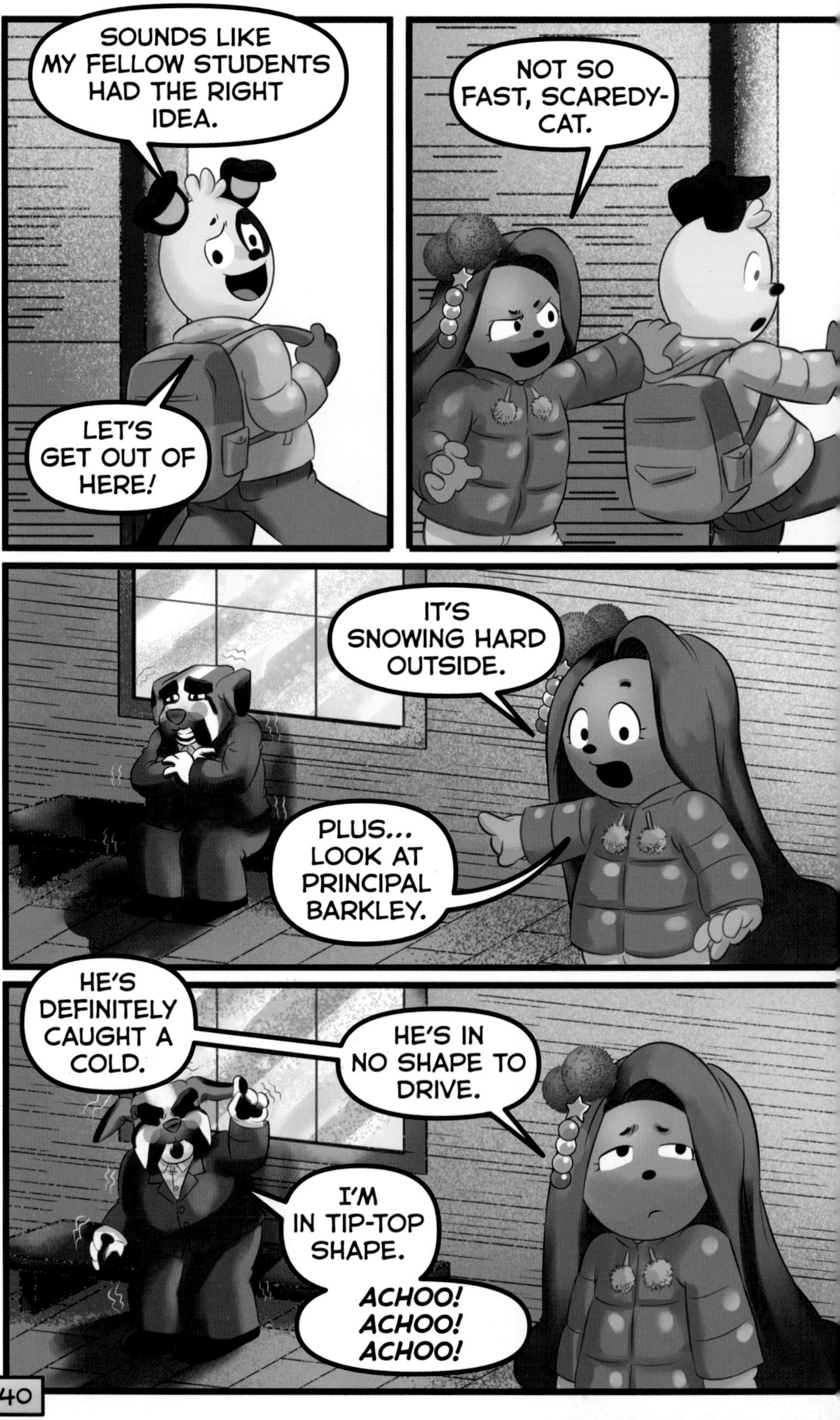
SOUNDS LIKE MY FELLOW STUDENTS HAD THE RIGHT IDEA.
LET'S GET OUT OF HERE!
NOT SO FAST, SCAREDY-CAT.
IT'S SNOWING HARD OUTSIDE.
PLUS... LOOK AT PRINCIPAL BARKLEY.
HE'S DEFINITELY CAUGHT A COLD.
HE'S IN NO SHAPE TO DRIVE.
I'M IN TIP-TOP SHAPE.
ACHOO! ACHOO! ACHOO!

GUS, PLEASE TAKE THEIR BAGS.

FINE.

OOOH. THAT GUY REALLY IS GRUMPY.

BET YOU HE IS THE BAD GUY.

MYSTERY SOLVED.

NOW CAN WE JUST FOCUS ON ROOM SERVICE AND NOT BOTHER WITH THE SNOWBOT?

NO!

43

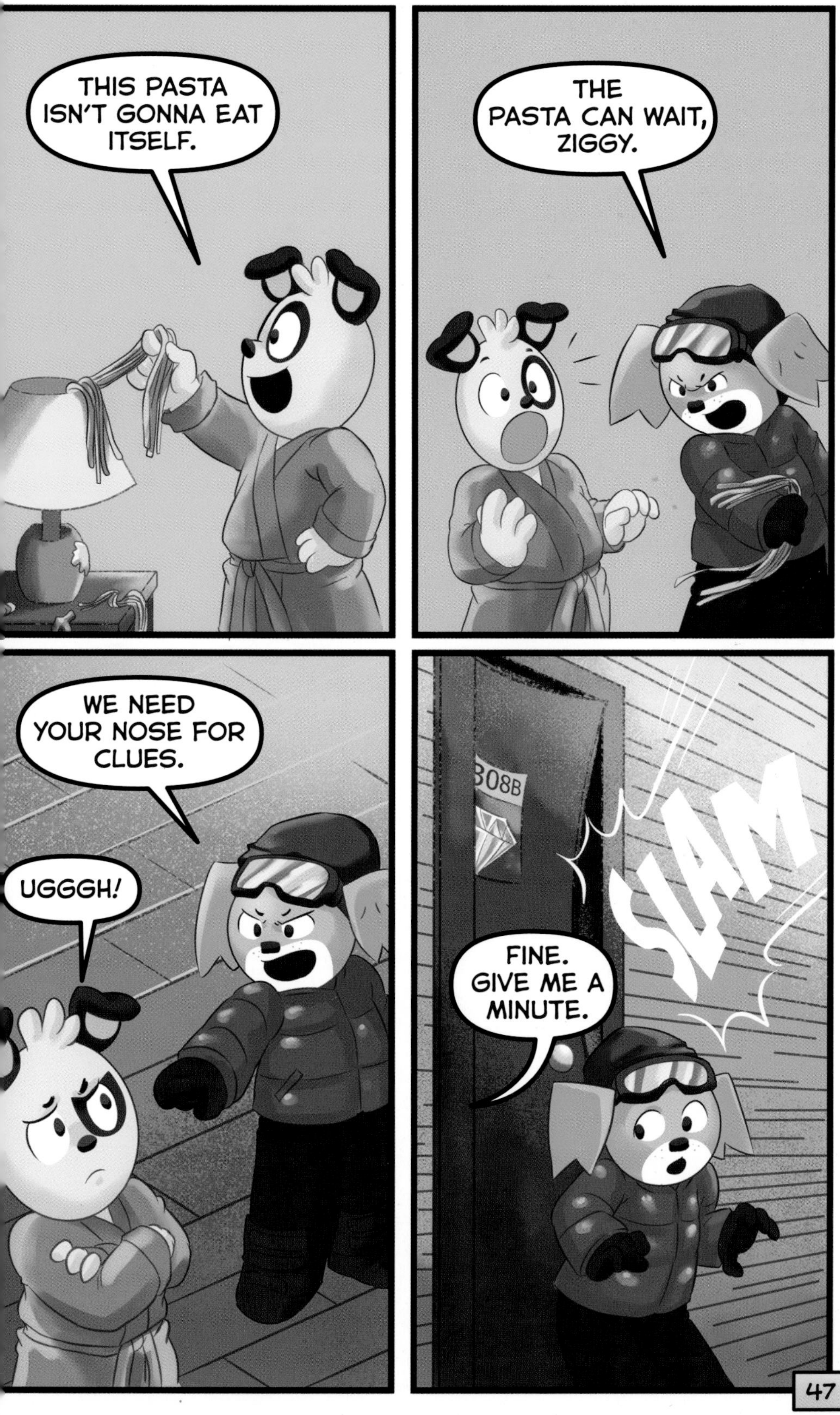
THIS PASTA ISN'T GONNA EAT ITSELF.
THE PASTA CAN WAIT, ZIGGY.
WE NEED YOUR NOSE FOR CLUES.
UGGGH!
308B
SLAM
FINE. GIVE ME A MINUTE.

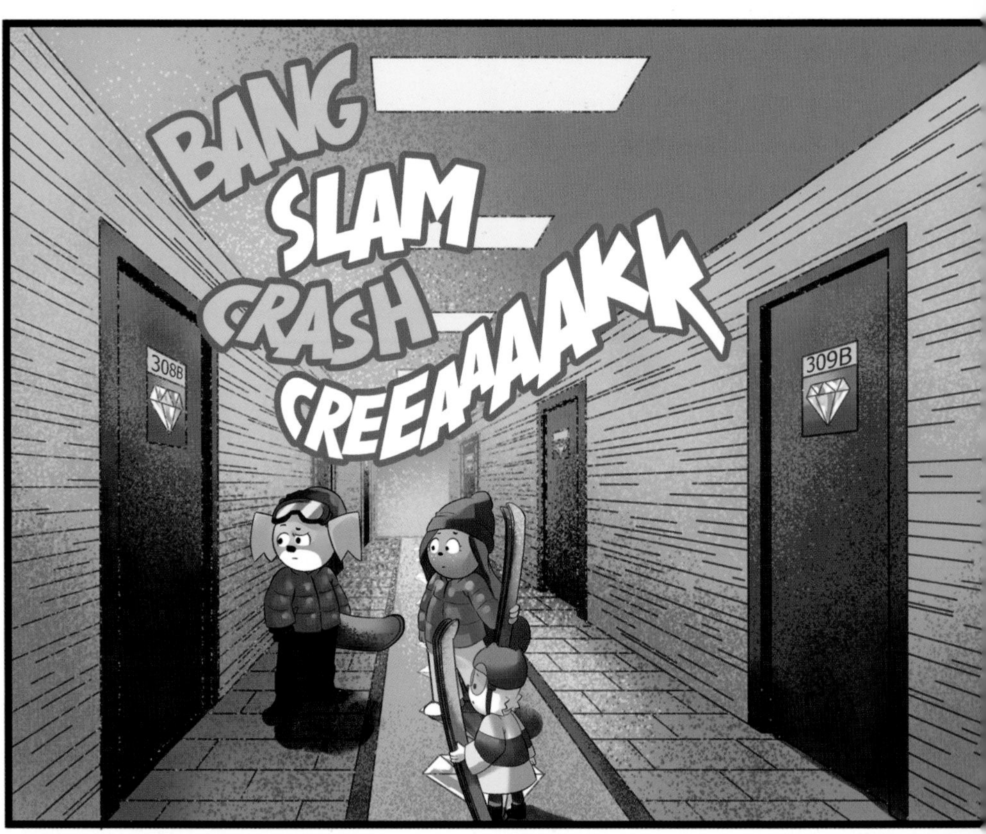
BANG
SLAM
CRASH
CREEAAAAKK
308B
309B

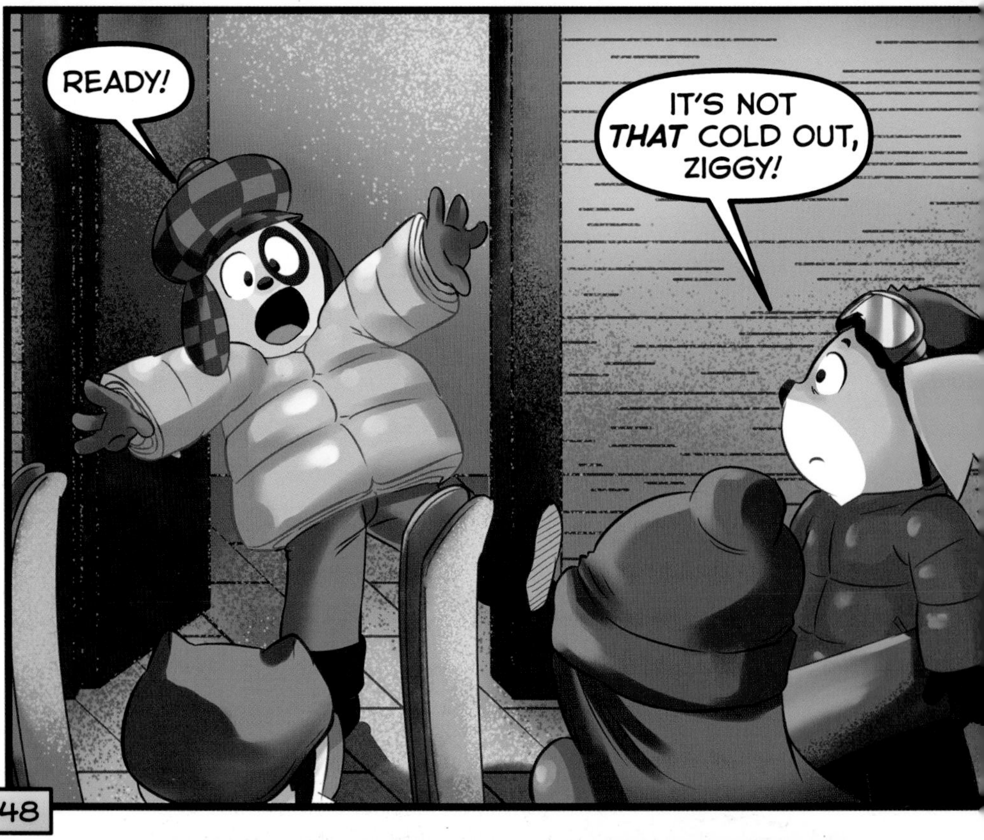
READY!
IT'S NOT *THAT* COLD OUT, ZIGGY!

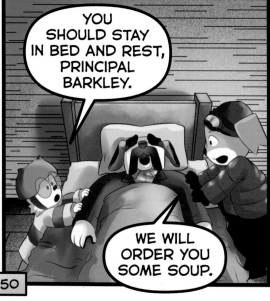

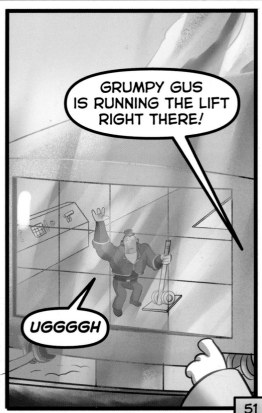

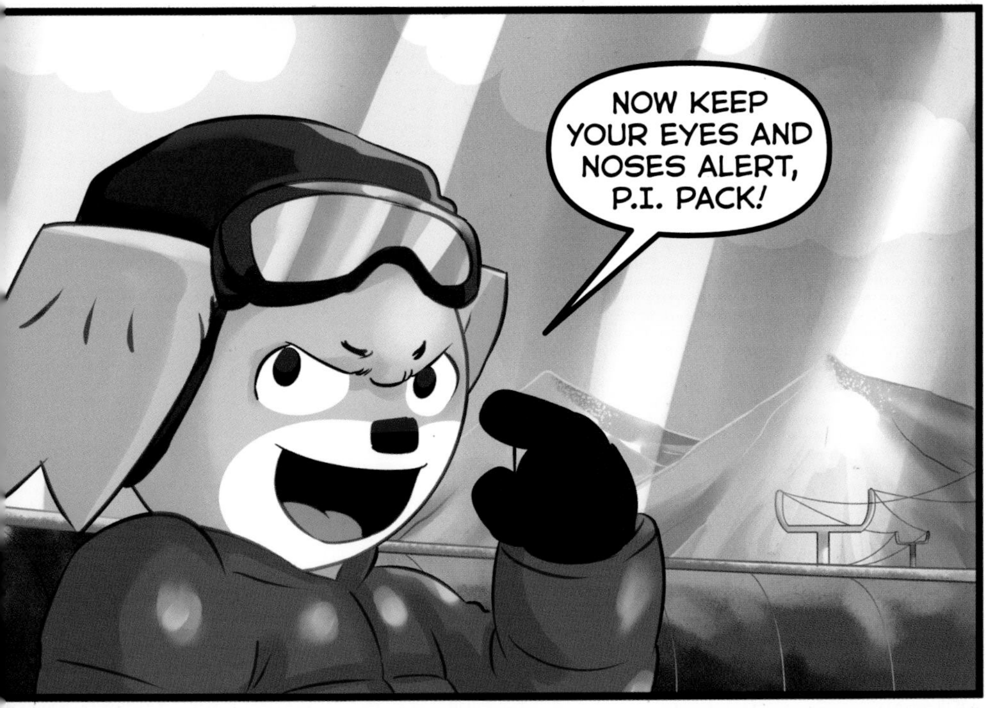
NOW KEEP YOUR EYES AND NOSES ALERT, P.I. PACK!

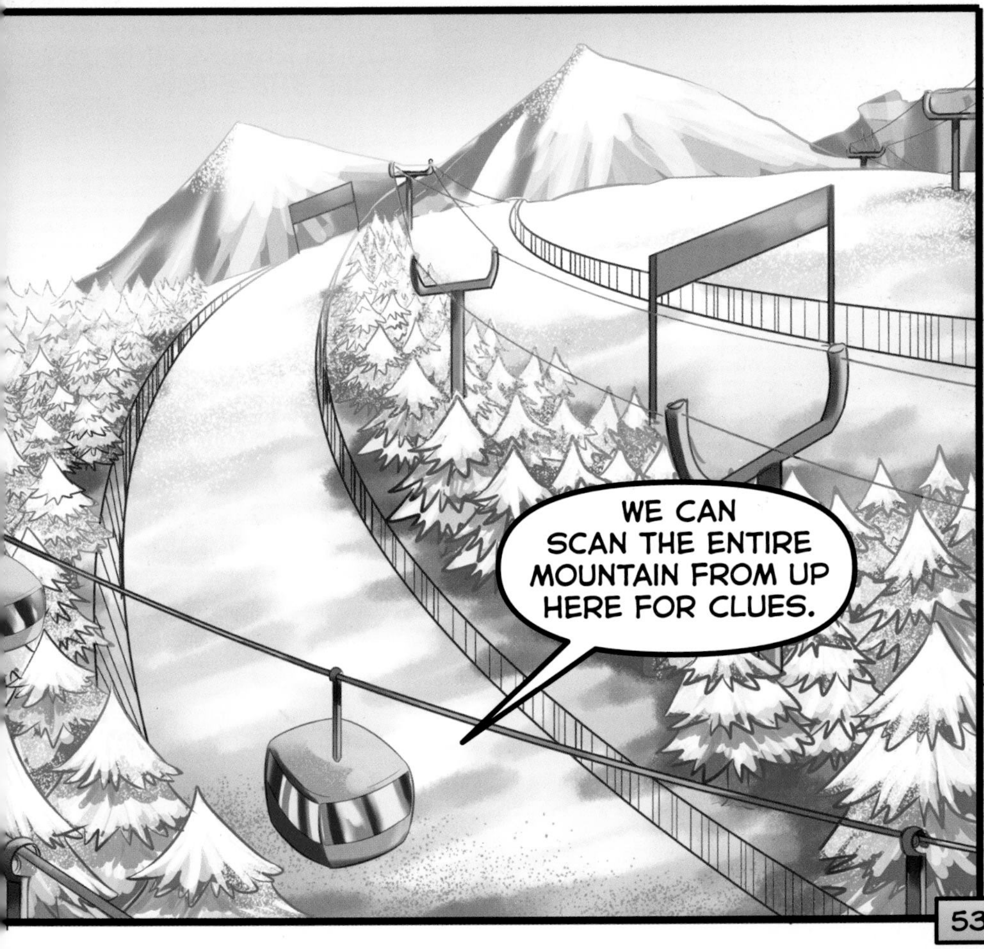
WE CAN SCAN THE ENTIRE MOUNTAIN FROM UP HERE FOR CLUES.

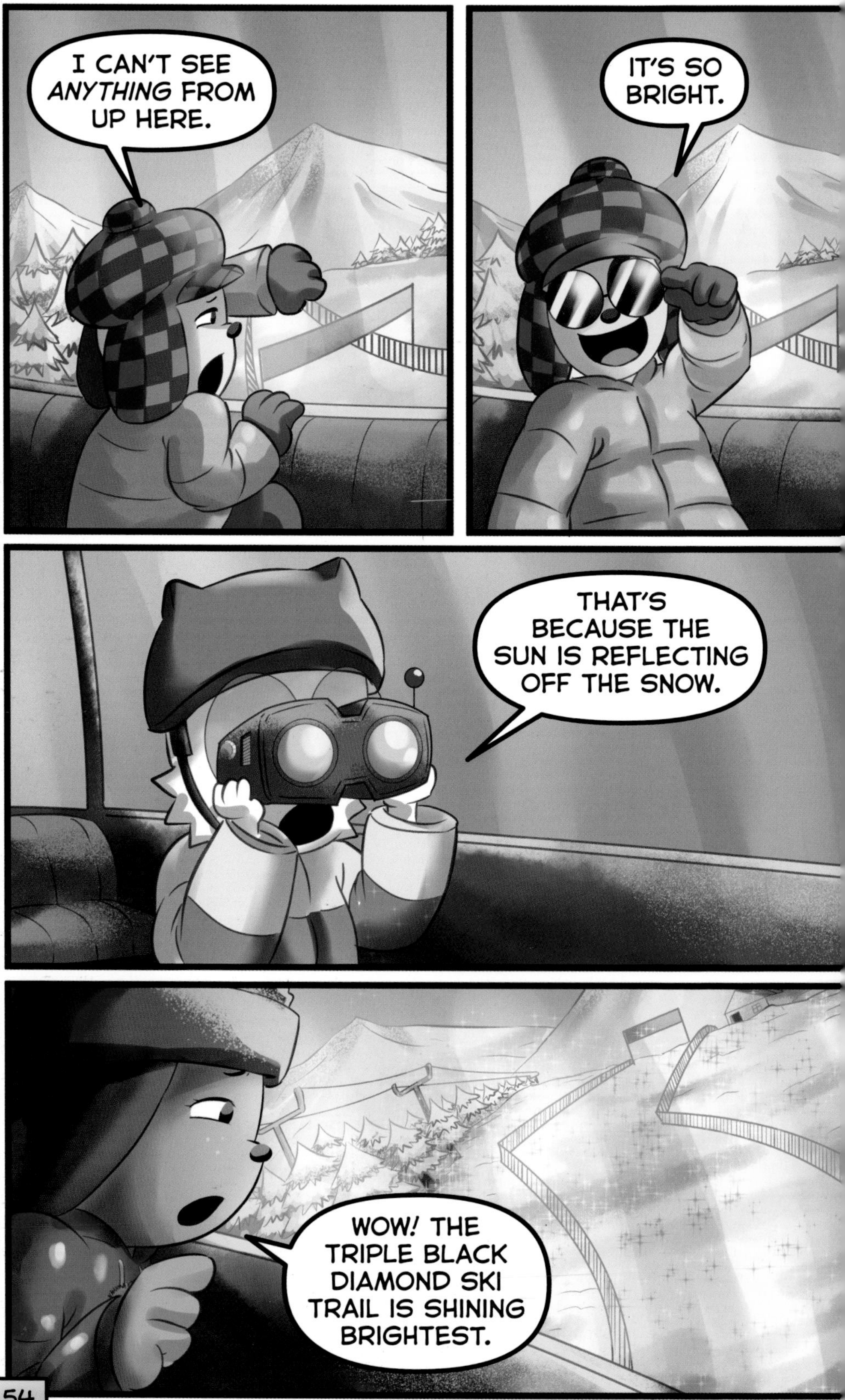
I CAN'T SEE *ANYTHING* FROM UP HERE.
IT'S SO BRIGHT.
THAT'S BECAUSE THE SUN IS REFLECTING OFF THE SNOW.
WOW! THE TRIPLE BLACK DIAMOND SKI TRAIL IS SHINING BRIGHTEST.

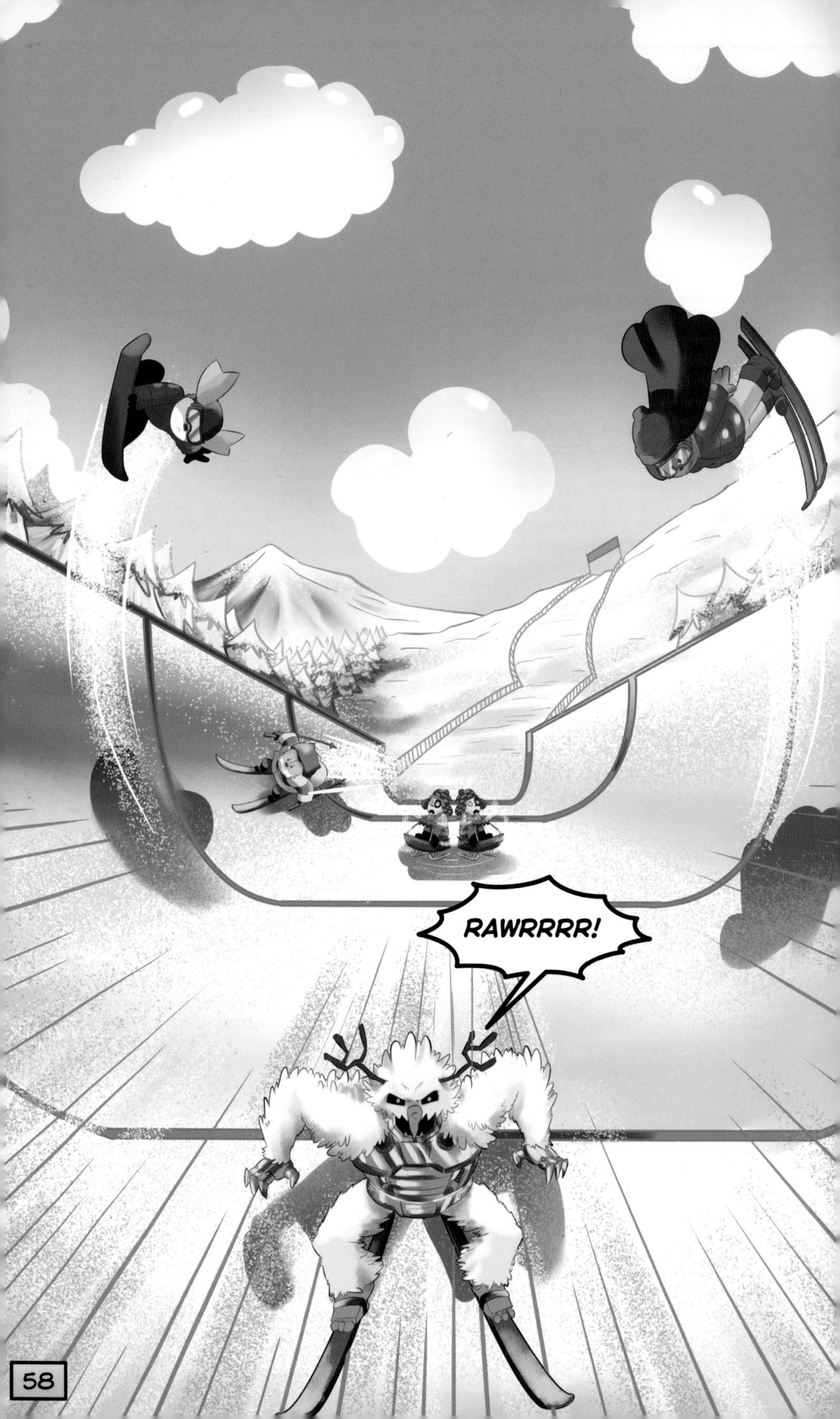
RAWRRRR!

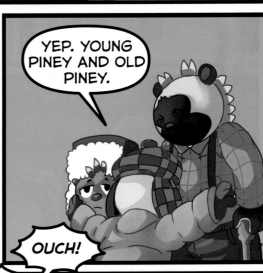

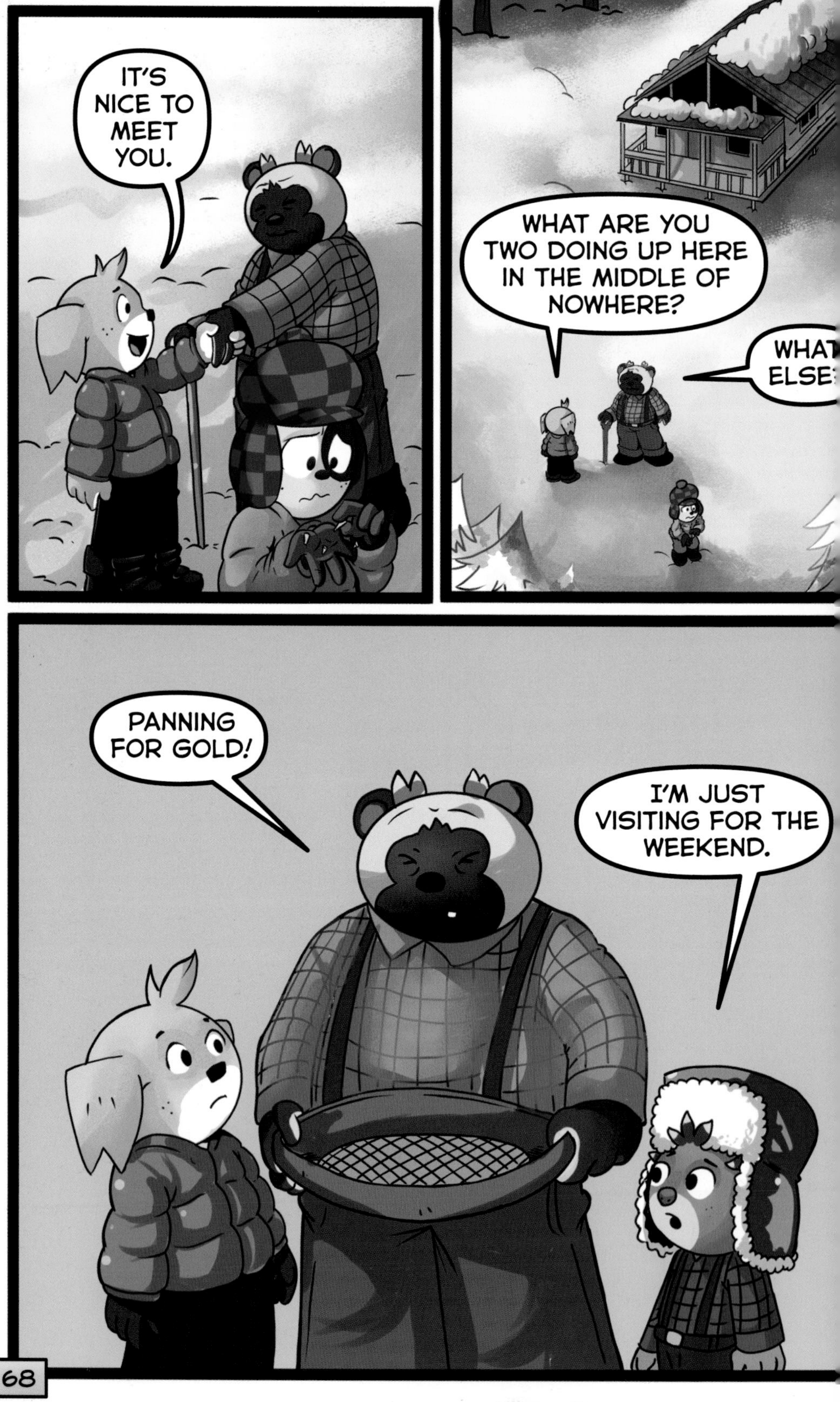
IT'S NICE TO MEET YOU.
WHAT ARE YOU TWO DOING UP HERE IN THE MIDDLE OF NOWHERE?
PANNING FOR GOLD!
I'M JUST VISITING FOR THE WEEKEND.

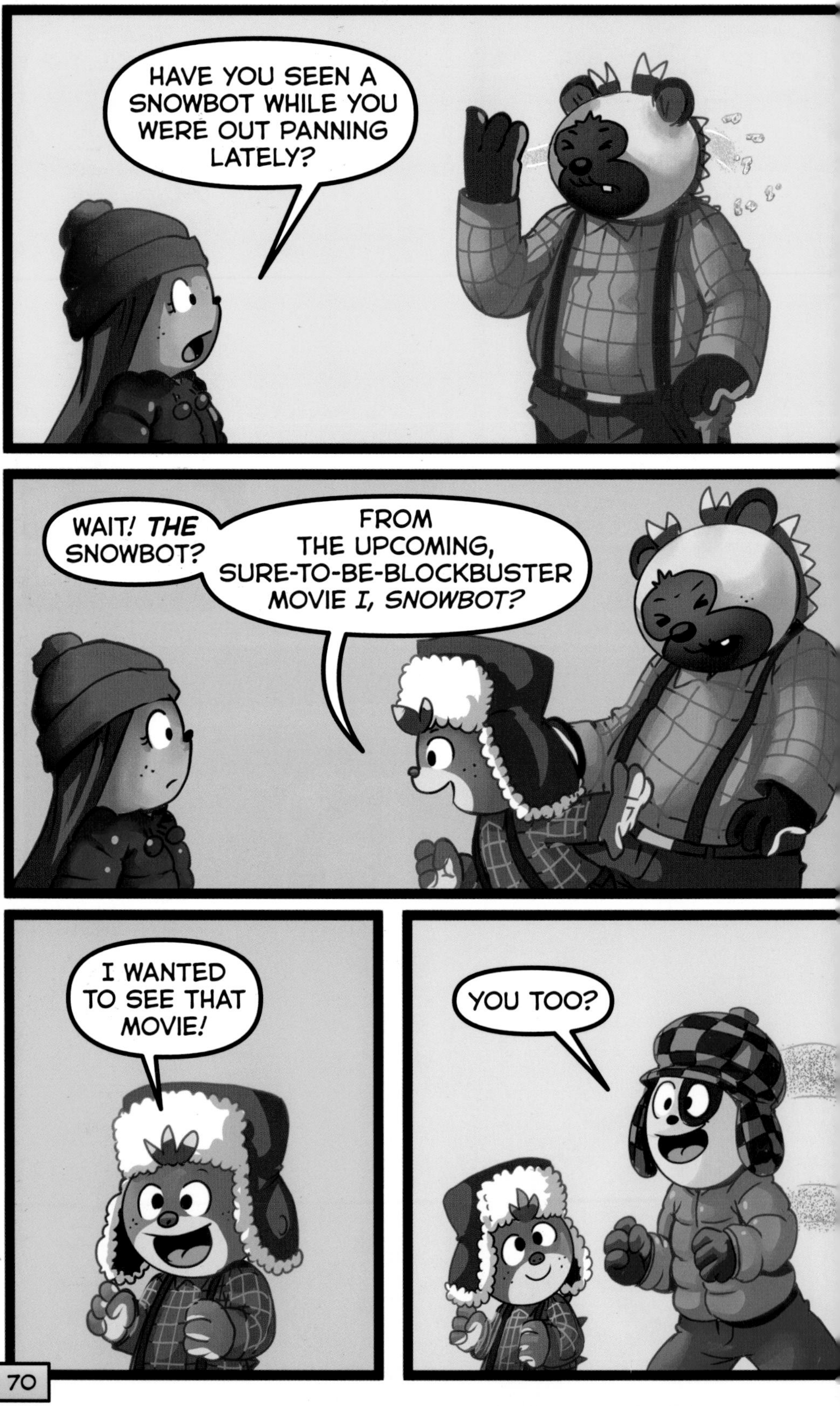
HAVE YOU SEEN A SNOWBOT WHILE YOU WERE OUT PANNING LATELY?
WAIT! *THE* SNOWBOT?
FROM THE UPCOMING, SURE-TO-BE-BLOCKBUSTER MOVIE *I, SNOWBOT?*
I WANTED TO SEE THAT MOVIE!
YOU TOO?

CHAPTER 6

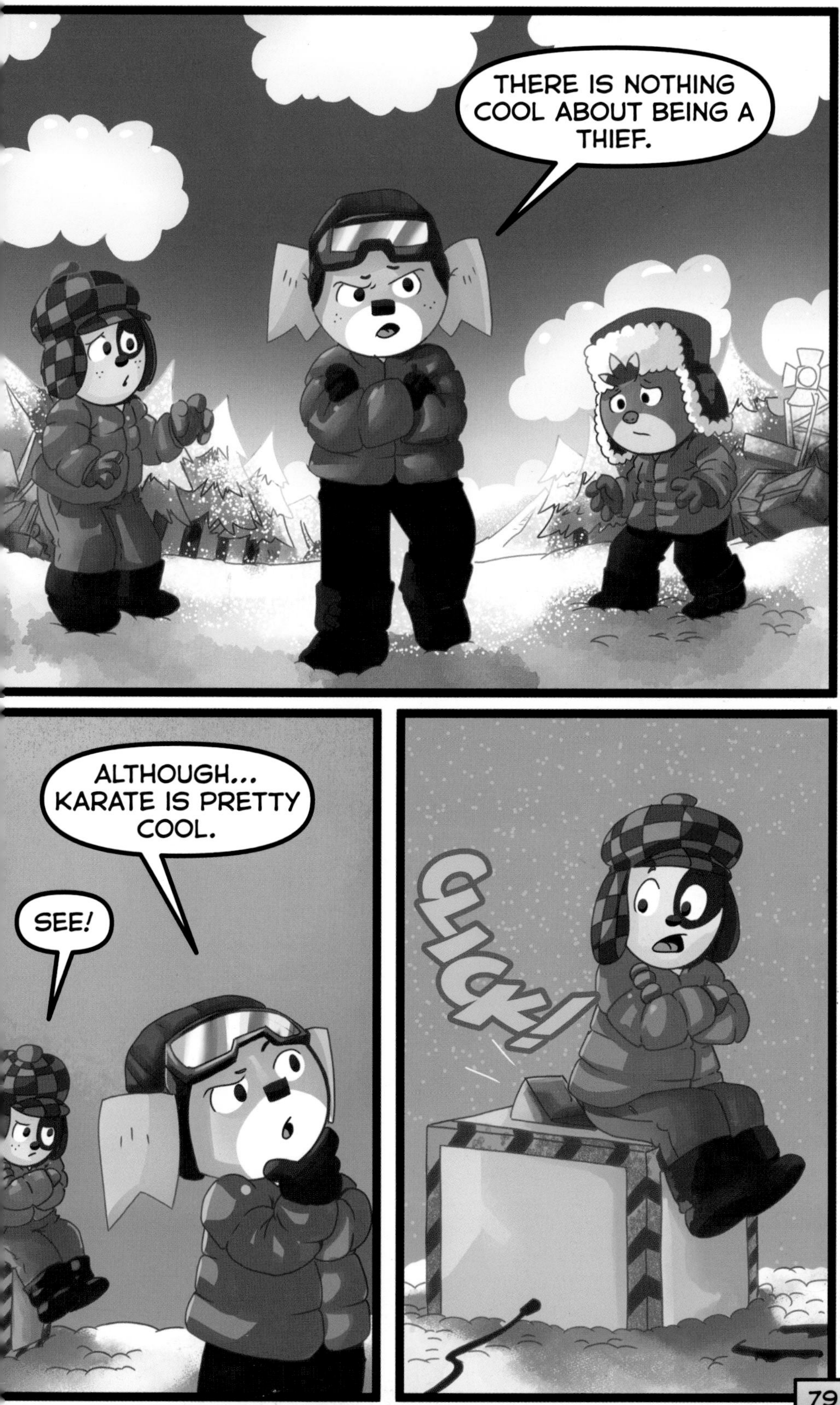
THERE IS NOTHING COOL ABOUT BEING A THIEF.
ALTHOUGH... KARATE IS PRETTY COOL.
SEE!
CLICK!

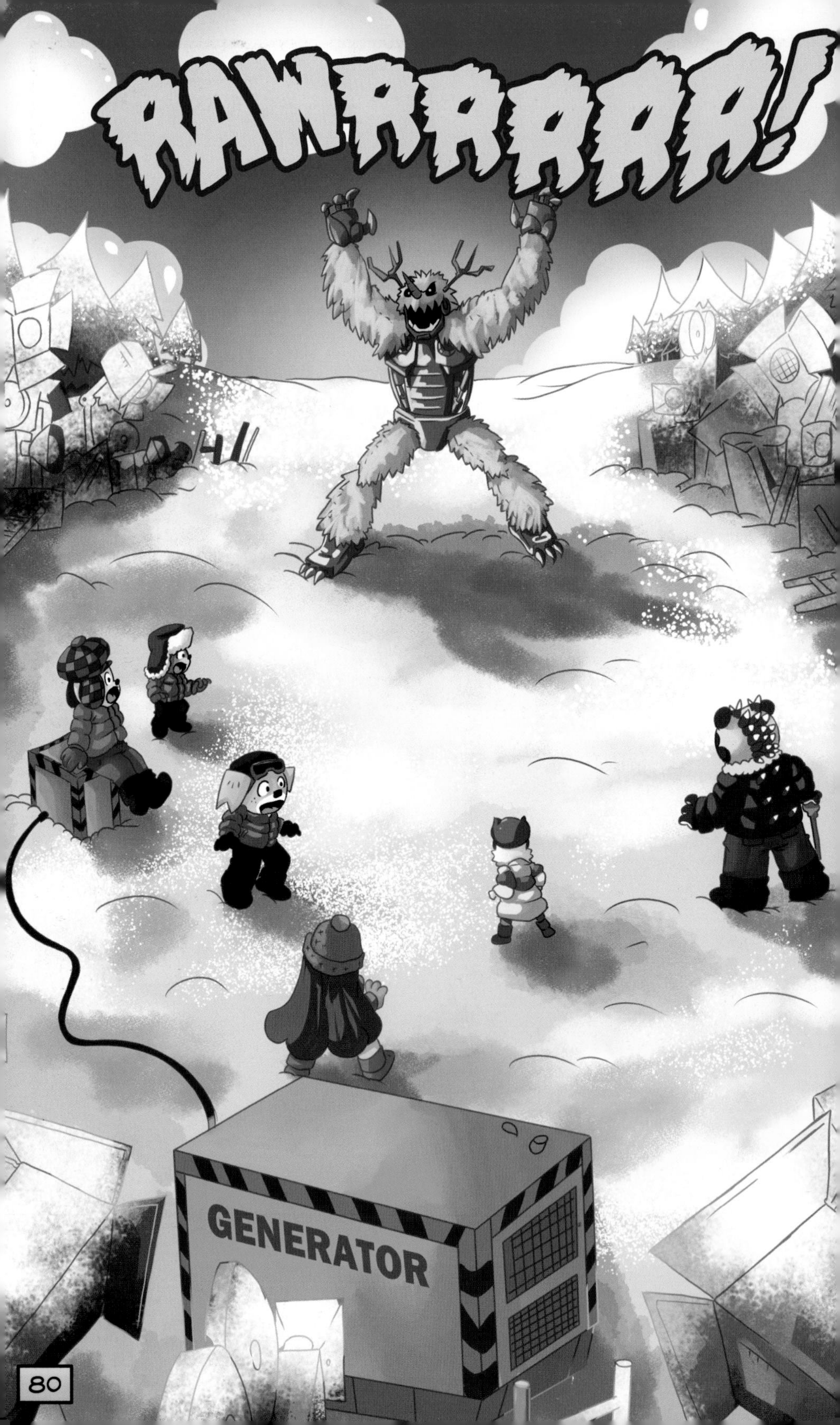
RAWRRRRR!
GENERATOR

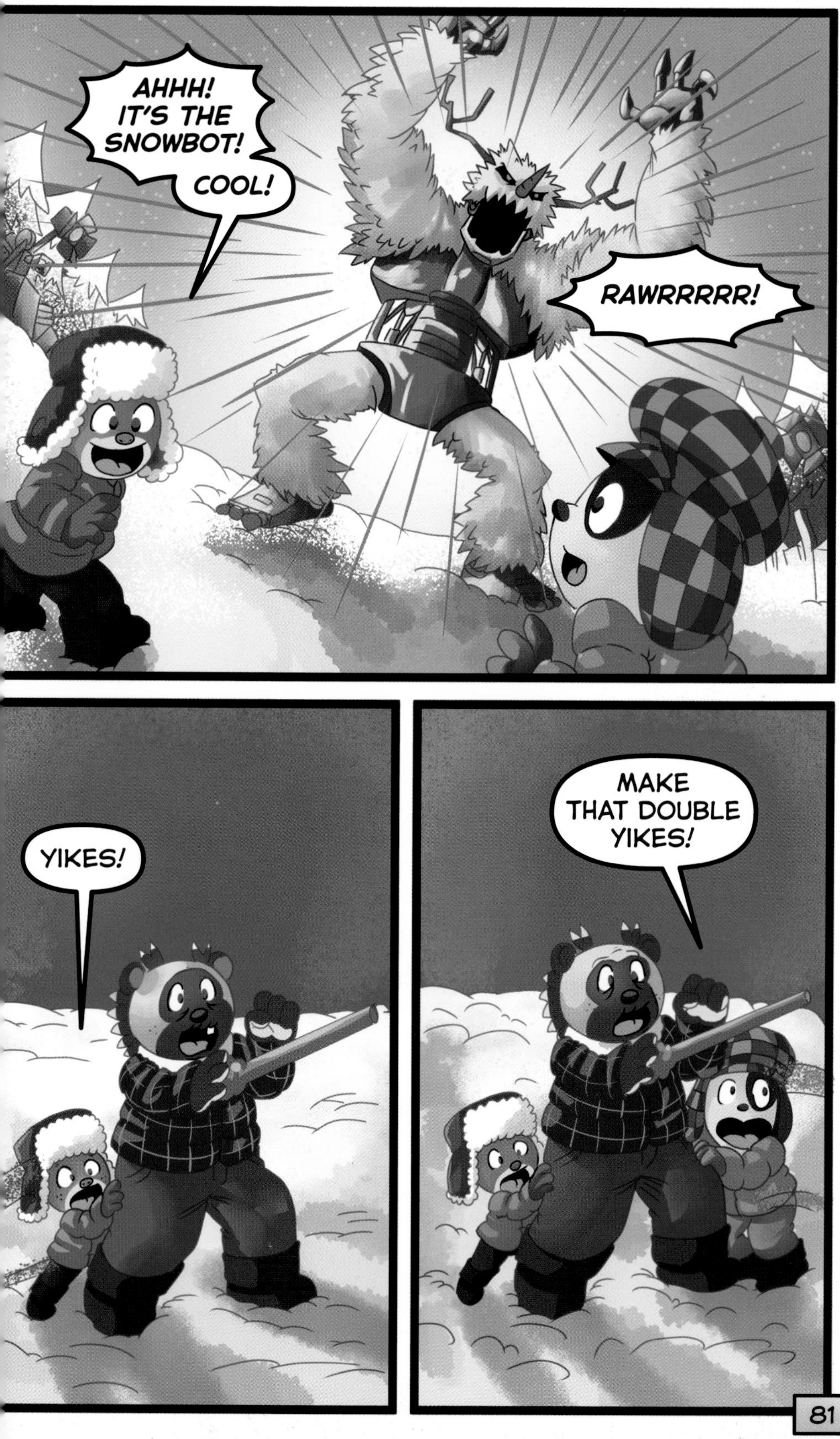
AHHH! IT'S THE SNOWBOT!
COOL!
RAWRRRRR!
YIKES!
MAKE THAT DOUBLE YIKES!

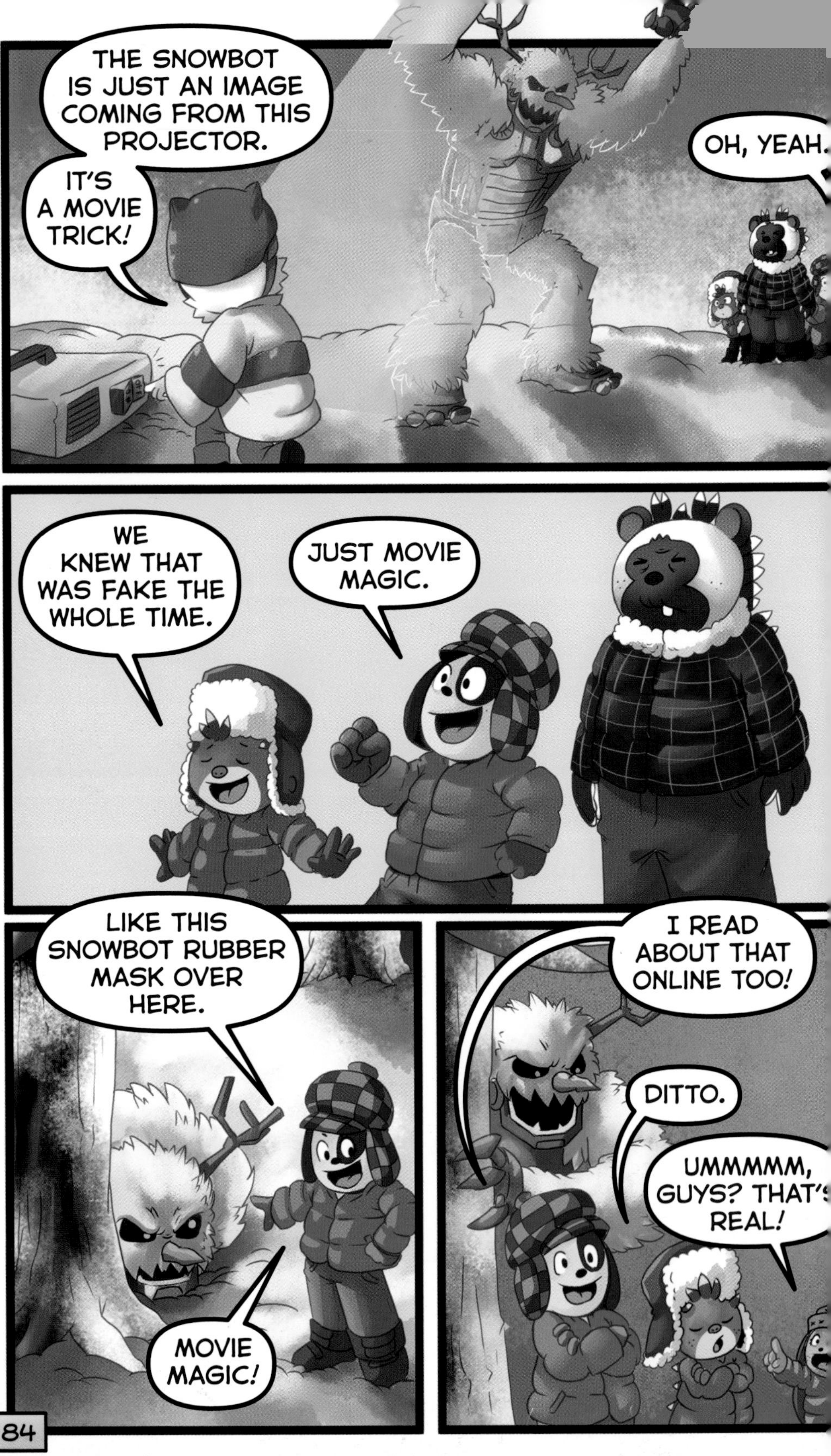
THE SNOWBOT IS JUST AN IMAGE COMING FROM THIS PROJECTOR.
IT'S A MOVIE TRICK!
OH, YEAH.
WE KNEW THAT WAS FAKE THE WHOLE TIME.
JUST MOVIE MAGIC.
LIKE THIS SNOWBOT RUBBER MASK OVER HERE.
MOVIE MAGIC!
I READ ABOUT THAT ONLINE TOO!
DITTO.
UMMMMM, GUYS? THAT'S REAL!

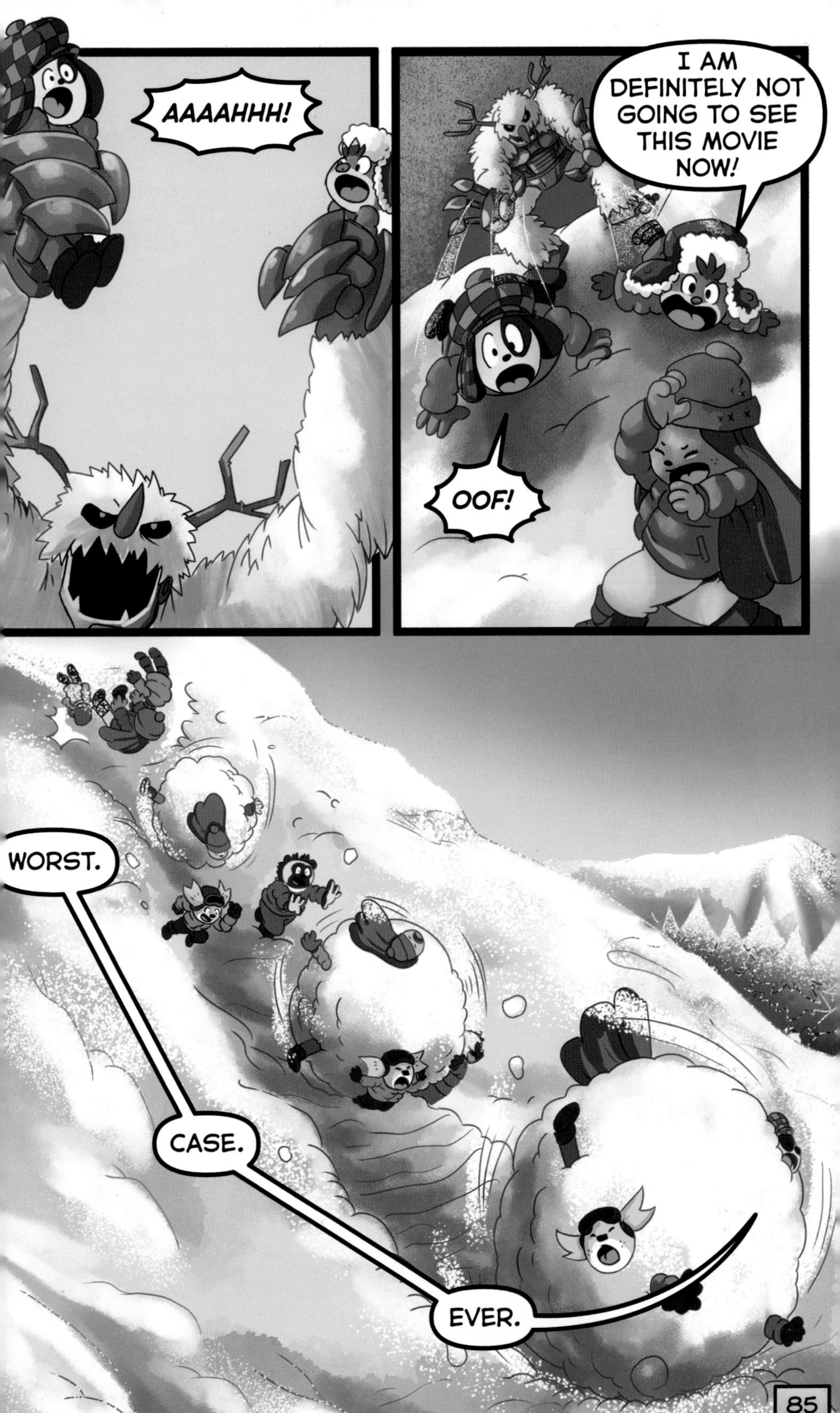
AAAAHHH!
I AM DEFINITELY NOT GOING TO SEE THIS MOVIE NOW!
OOF!
WORST.
CASE.
EVER.

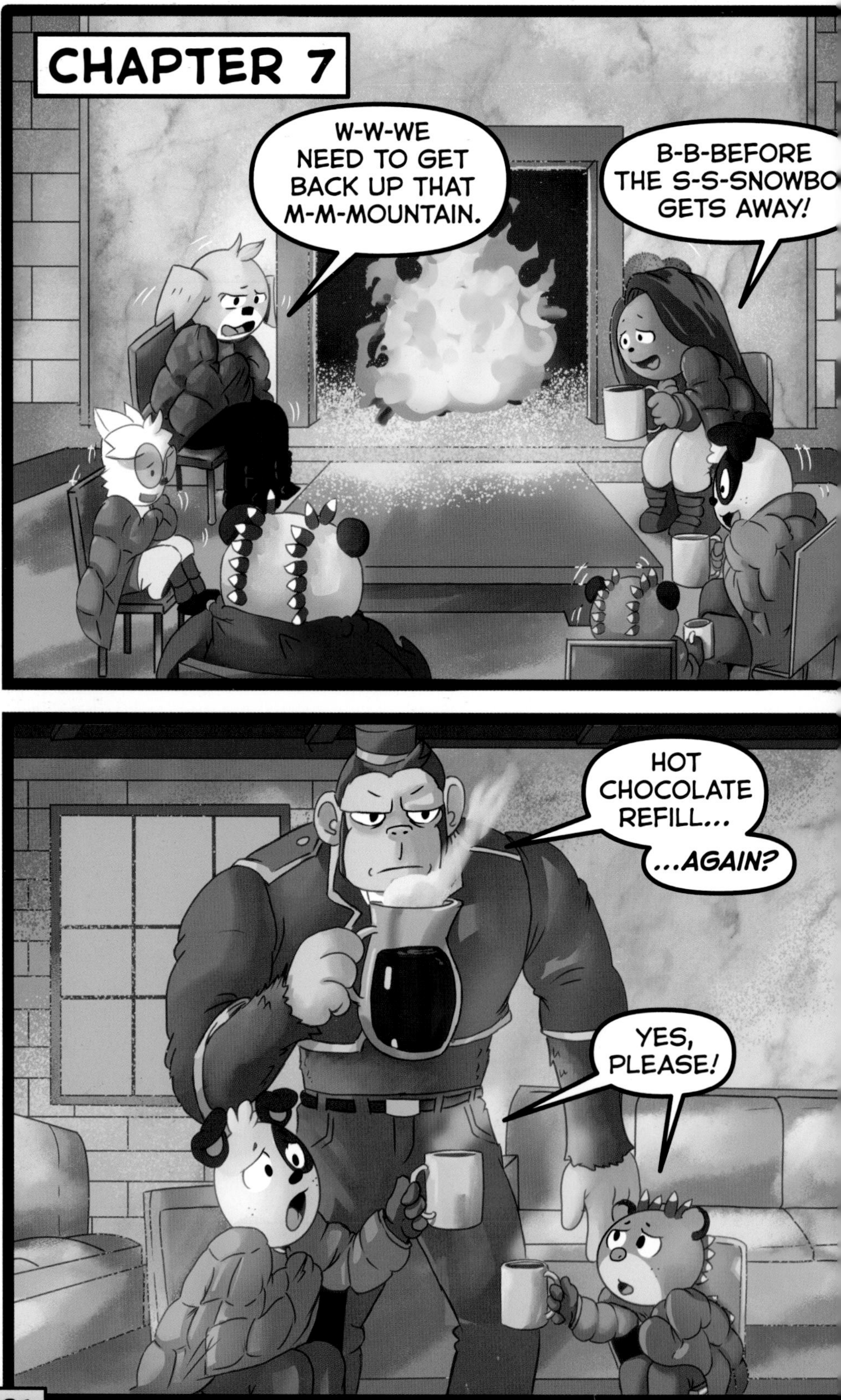
CHAPTER 7
W-W-WE NEED TO GET BACK UP THAT M-M-MOUNTAIN.
B-B-BEFORE THE S-S-SNOWBO GETS AWAY!
HOT CHOCOLATE REFILL... ...AGAIN?
YES, PLEASE!

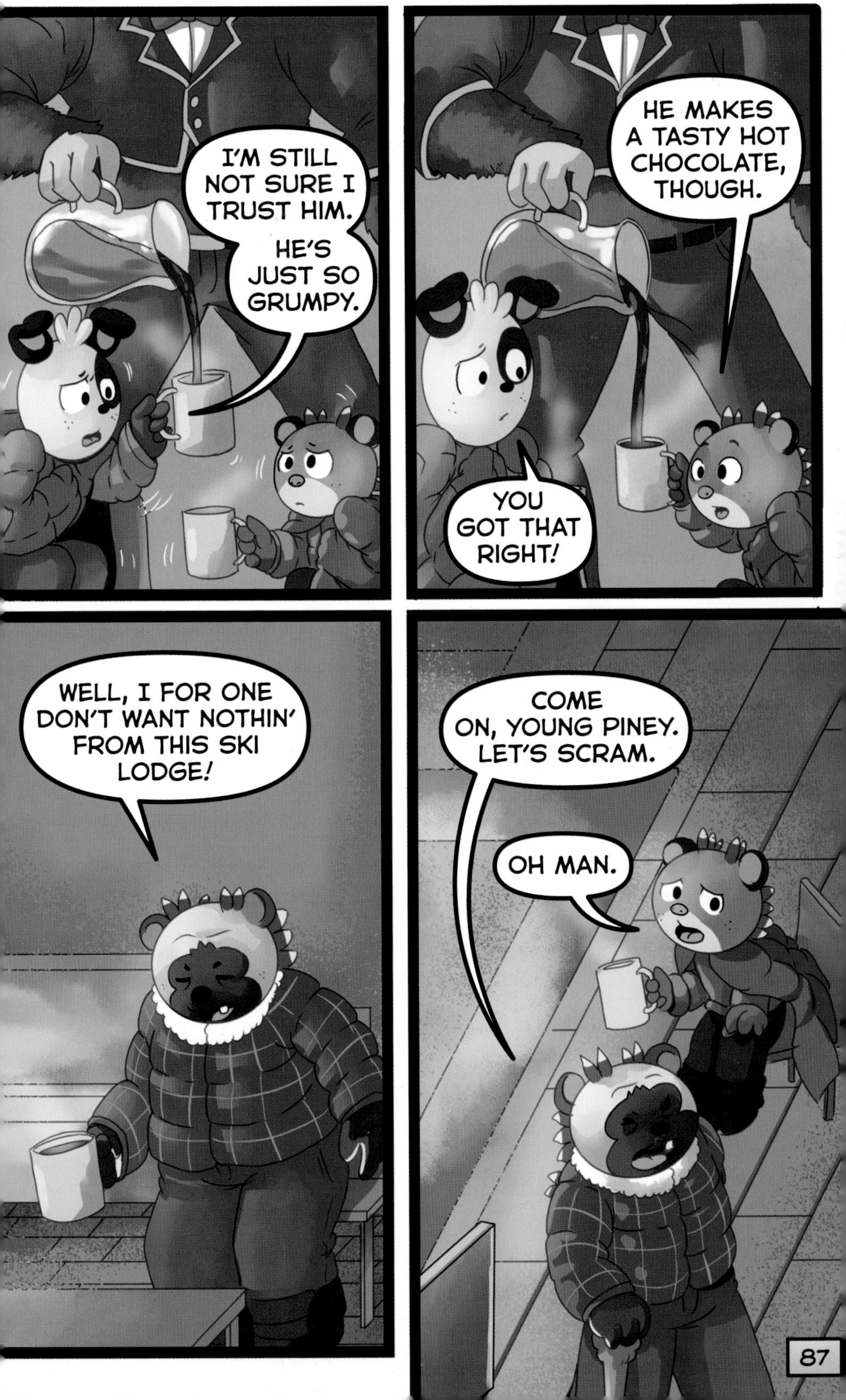

I'M STILL NOT SURE I TRUST HIM.
HE'S JUST SO GRUMPY.
HE MAKES A TASTY HOT CHOCOLATE, THOUGH.
YOU GOT THAT RIGHT!
WELL, I FOR ONE DON'T WANT NOTHIN' FROM THIS SKI LODGE!
COME ON, YOUNG PINEY. LET'S SCRAM.
OH MAN.

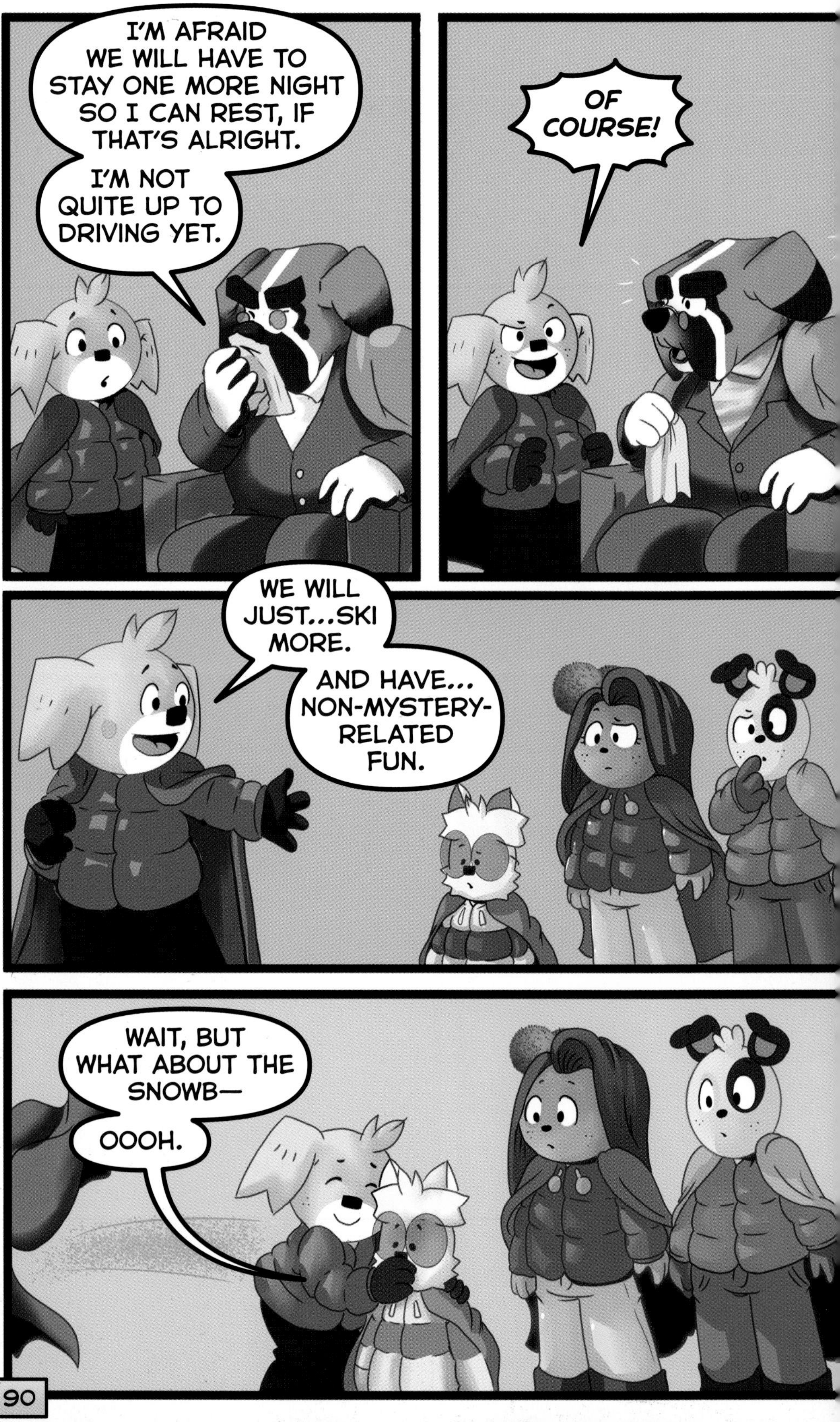
I'M AFRAID WE WILL HAVE TO STAY ONE MORE NIGHT SO I CAN REST, IF THAT'S ALRIGHT.
I'M NOT QUITE UP TO DRIVING YET.
OF COURSE!
WE WILL JUST...SKI MORE.
AND HAVE... NON-MYSTERY-RELATED FUN.
WAIT, BUT WHAT ABOUT THE SNOWB—
OOOH.

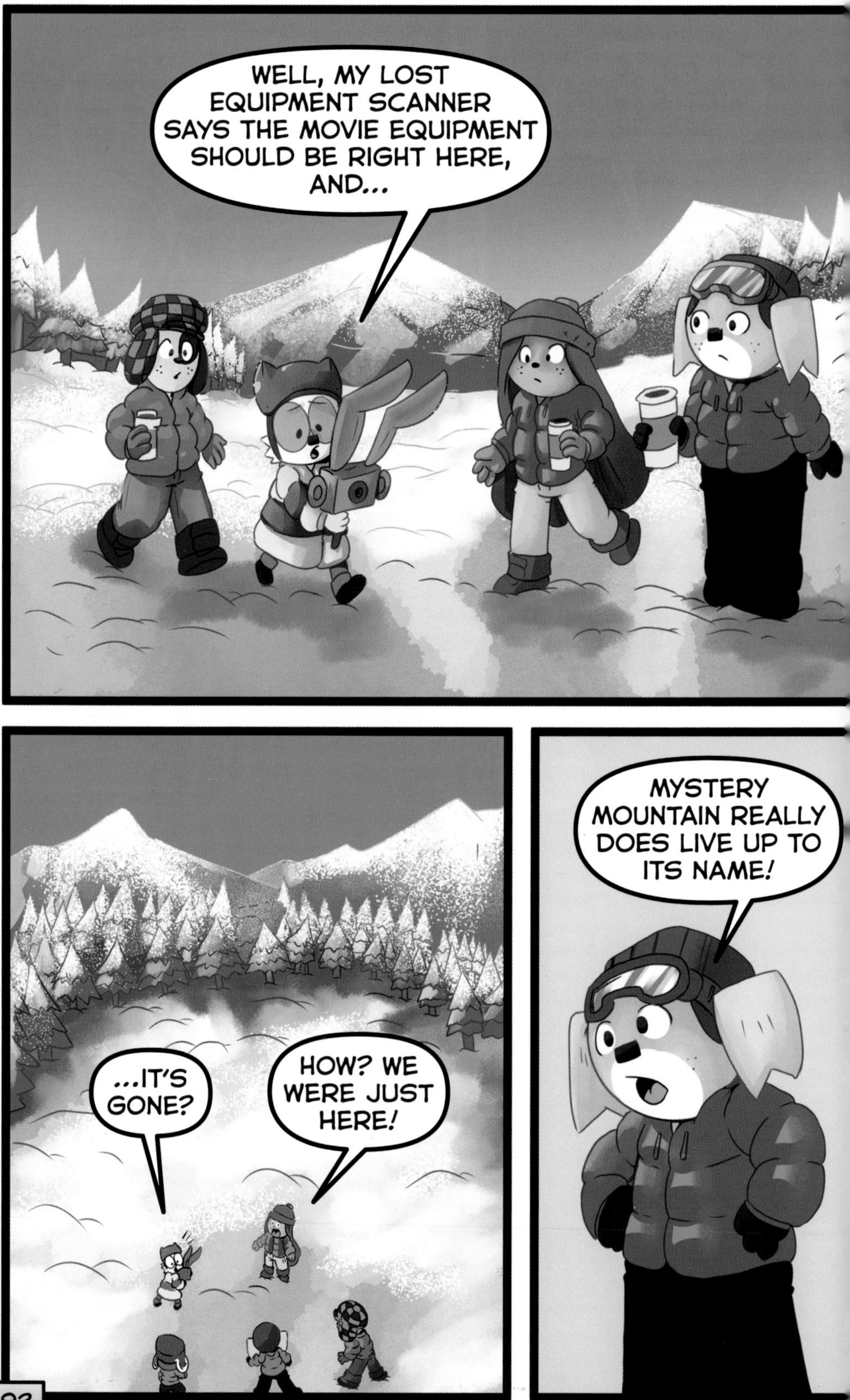
WELL, MY LOST EQUIPMENT SCANNER SAYS THE MOVIE EQUIPMENT SHOULD BE RIGHT HERE, AND...
...IT'S GONE?
HOW? WE WERE JUST HERE!
MYSTERY MOUNTAIN REALLY DOES LIVE UP TO ITS NAME!

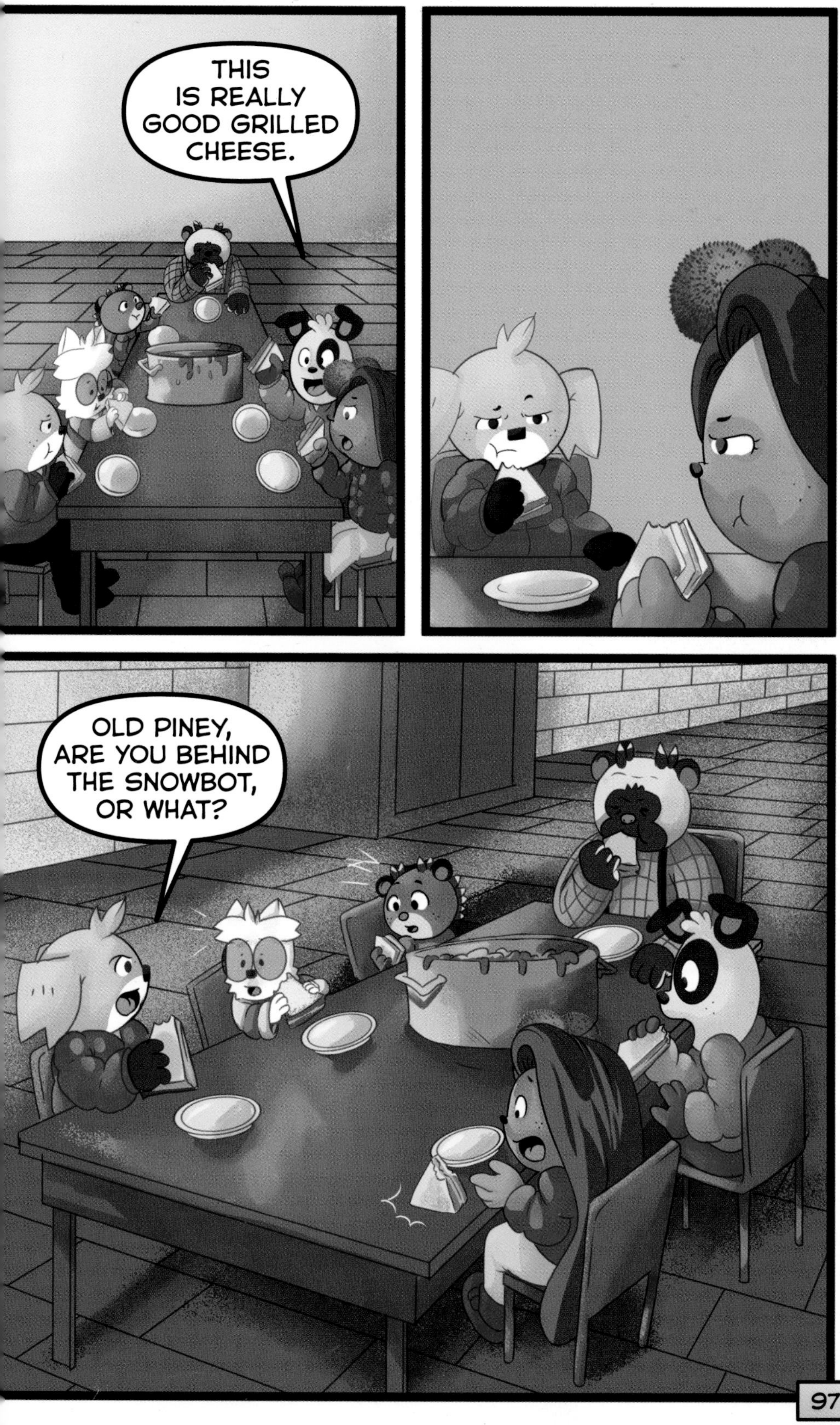
THIS IS REALLY GOOD GRILLED CHEESE.
OLD PINEY, ARE YOU BEHIND THE SNOWBOT, OR WHAT?

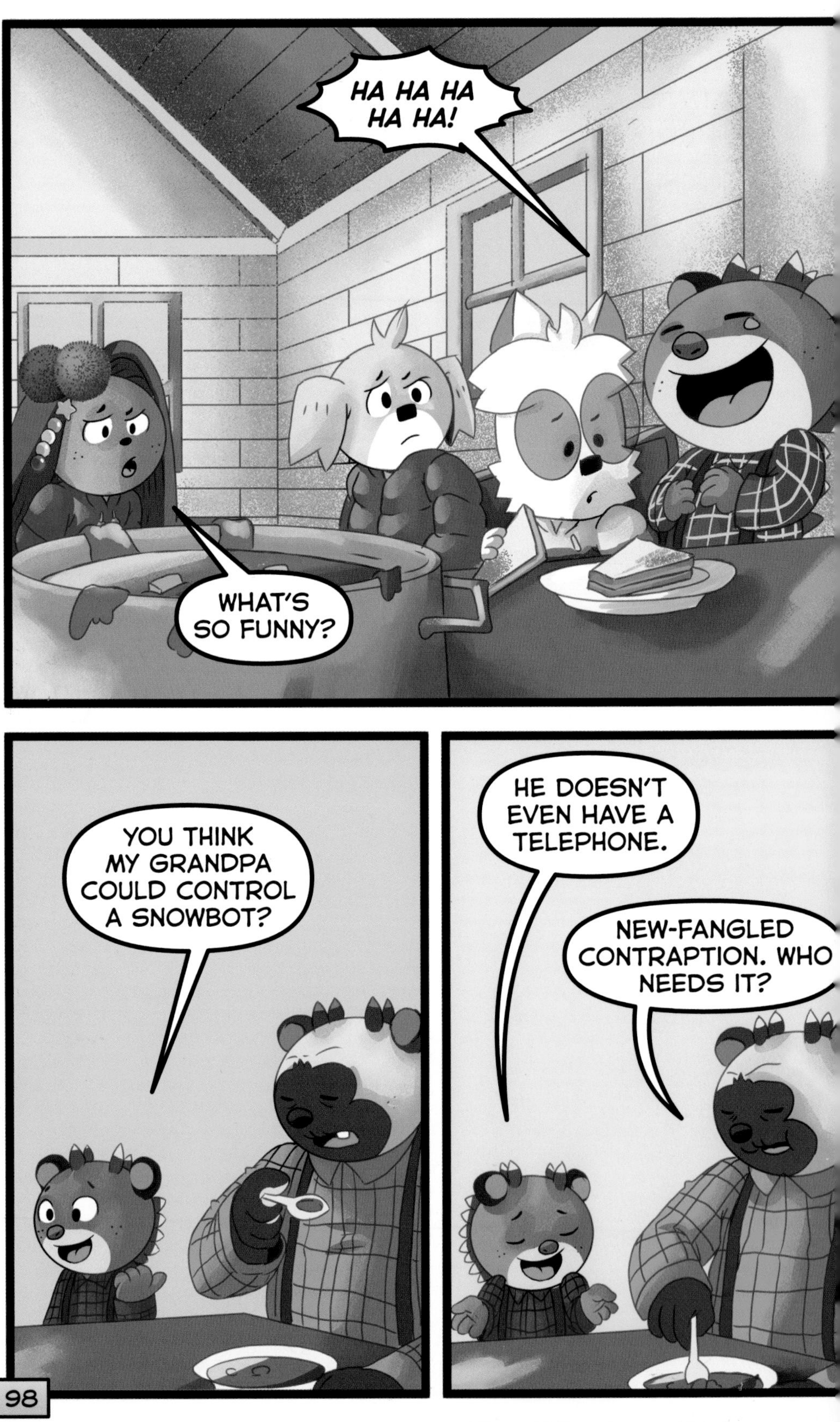
HA HA HA
HA HA!
WHAT'S SO FUNNY?
YOU THINK MY GRANDPA COULD CONTROL A SNOWBOT?
HE DOESN'T EVEN HAVE A TELEPHONE.
NEW-FANGLED CONTRAPTION. WHO NEEDS IT?

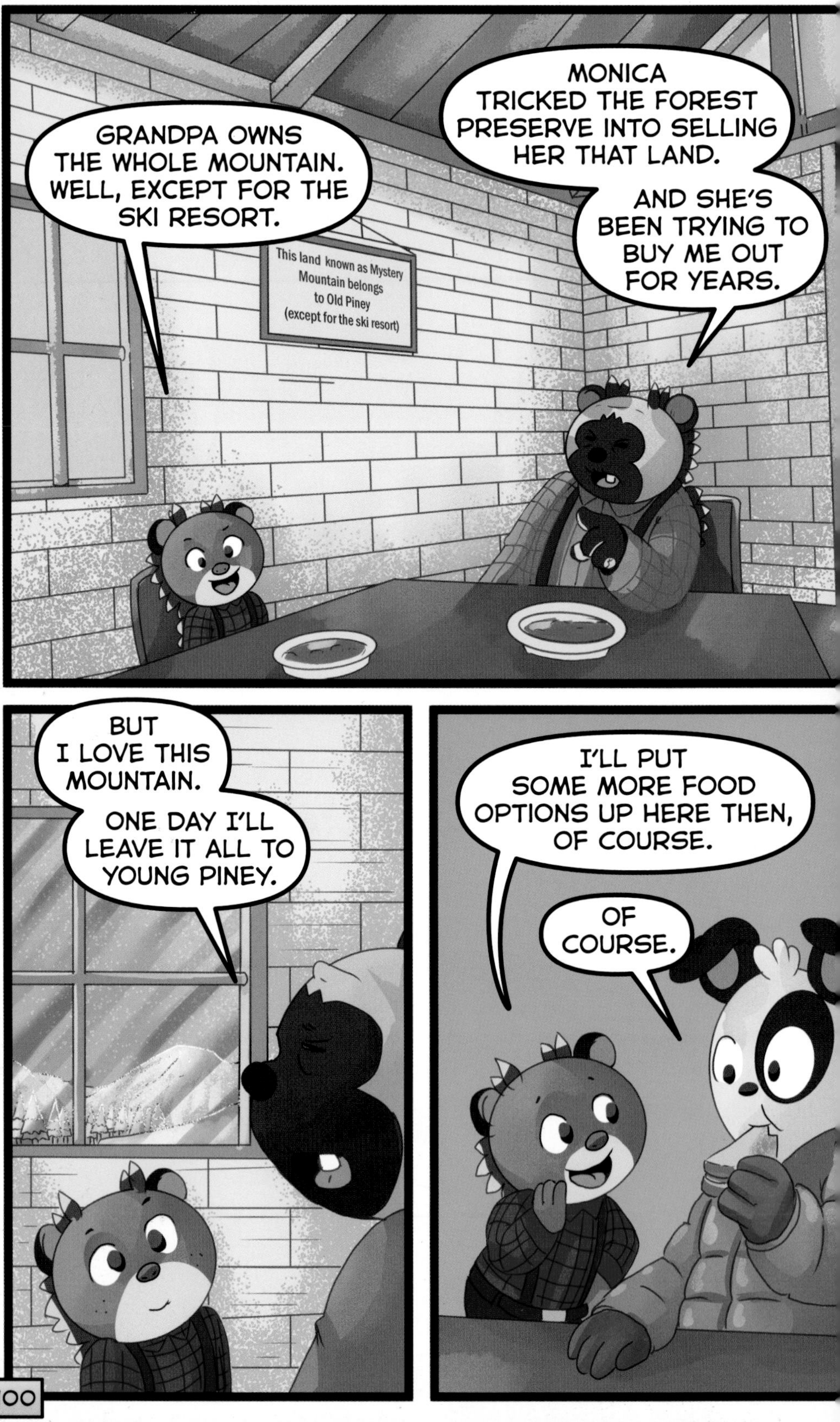
GRANDPA OWNS THE WHOLE MOUNTAIN. WELL, EXCEPT FOR THE SKI RESORT.
This land known as Mystery Mountain belongs to Old Piney (except for the ski resort)
MONICA TRICKED THE FOREST PRESERVE INTO SELLING HER THAT LAND.
AND SHE'S BEEN TRYING TO BUY ME OUT FOR YEARS.
BUT I LOVE THIS MOUNTAIN.
ONE DAY I'LL LEAVE IT ALL TO YOUNG PINEY.
I'LL PUT SOME MORE FOOD OPTIONS UP HERE THEN, OF COURSE.
OF COURSE.

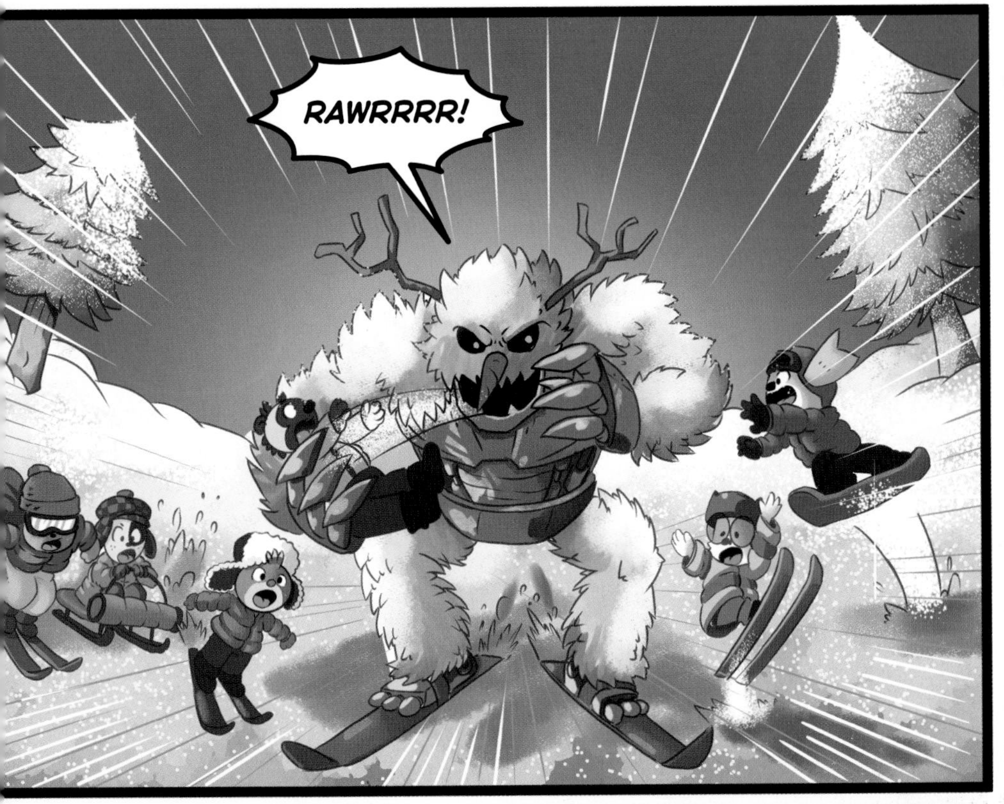
RAWRRRR!
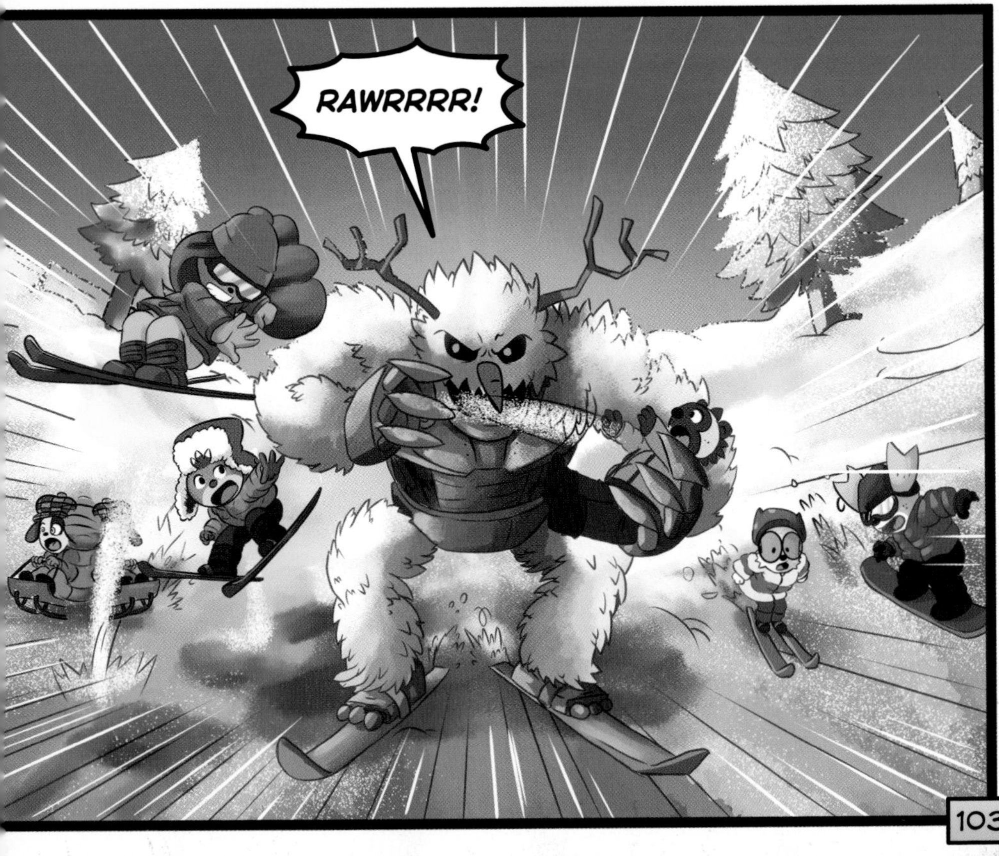
RAWRRRR!

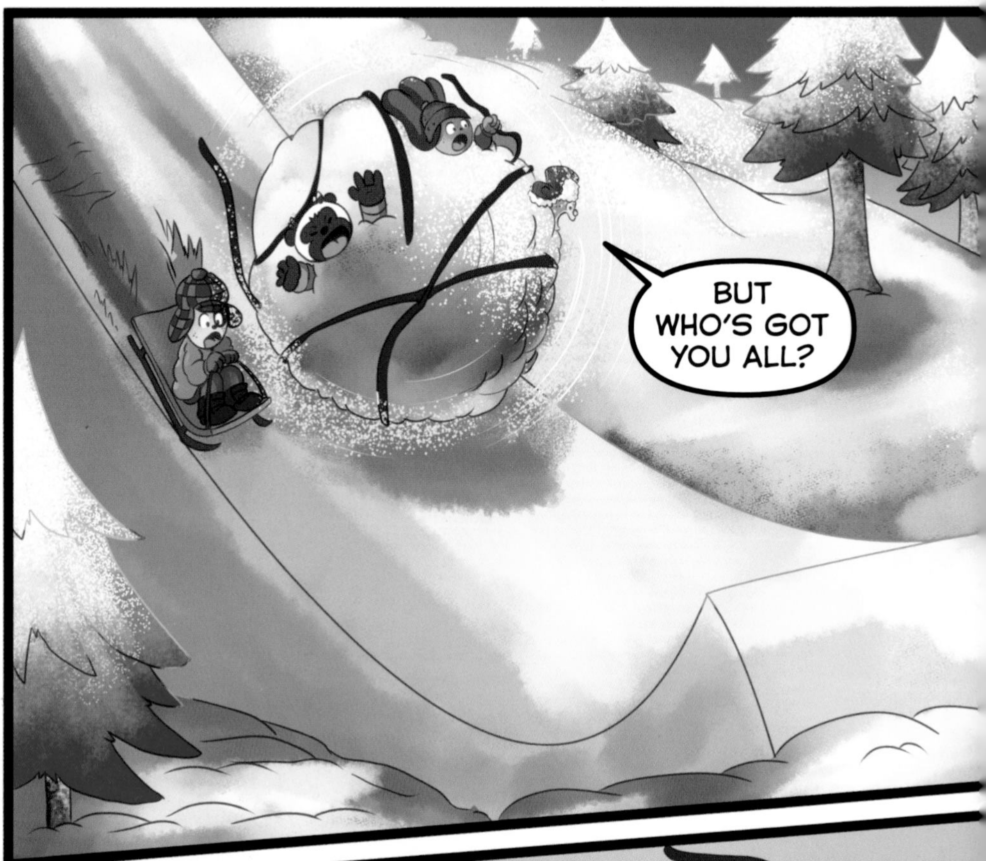
BUT WHO'S GOT YOU ALL?

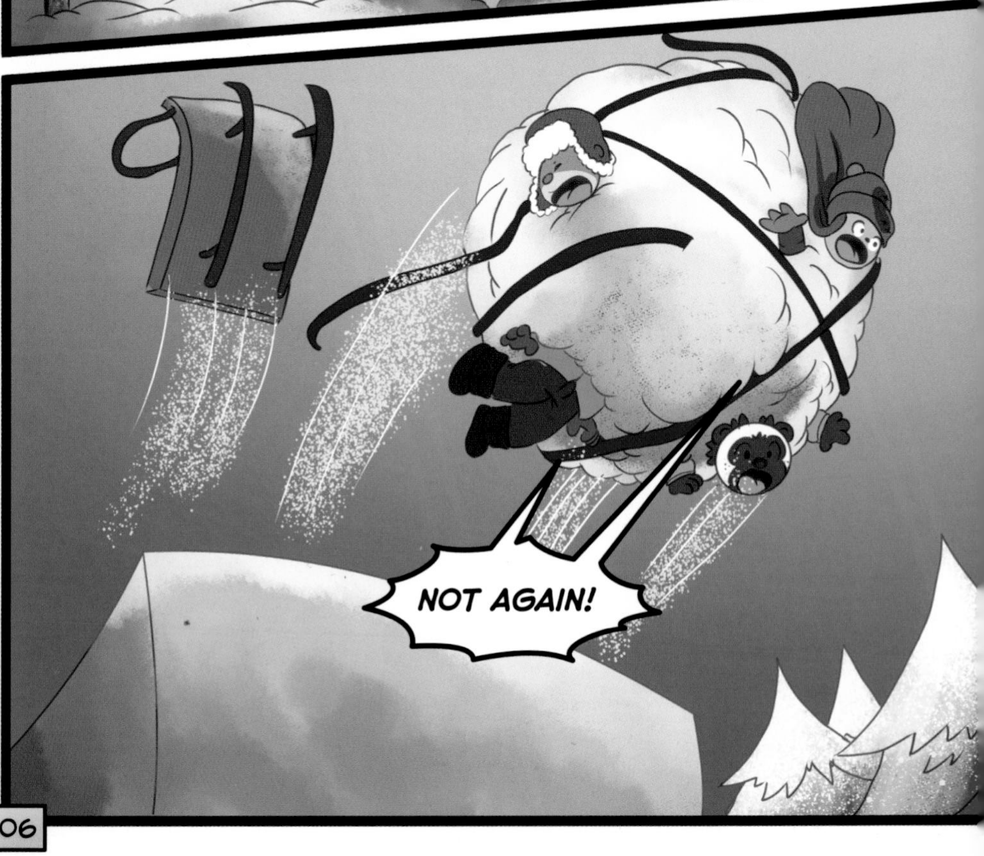
NOT AGAIN!

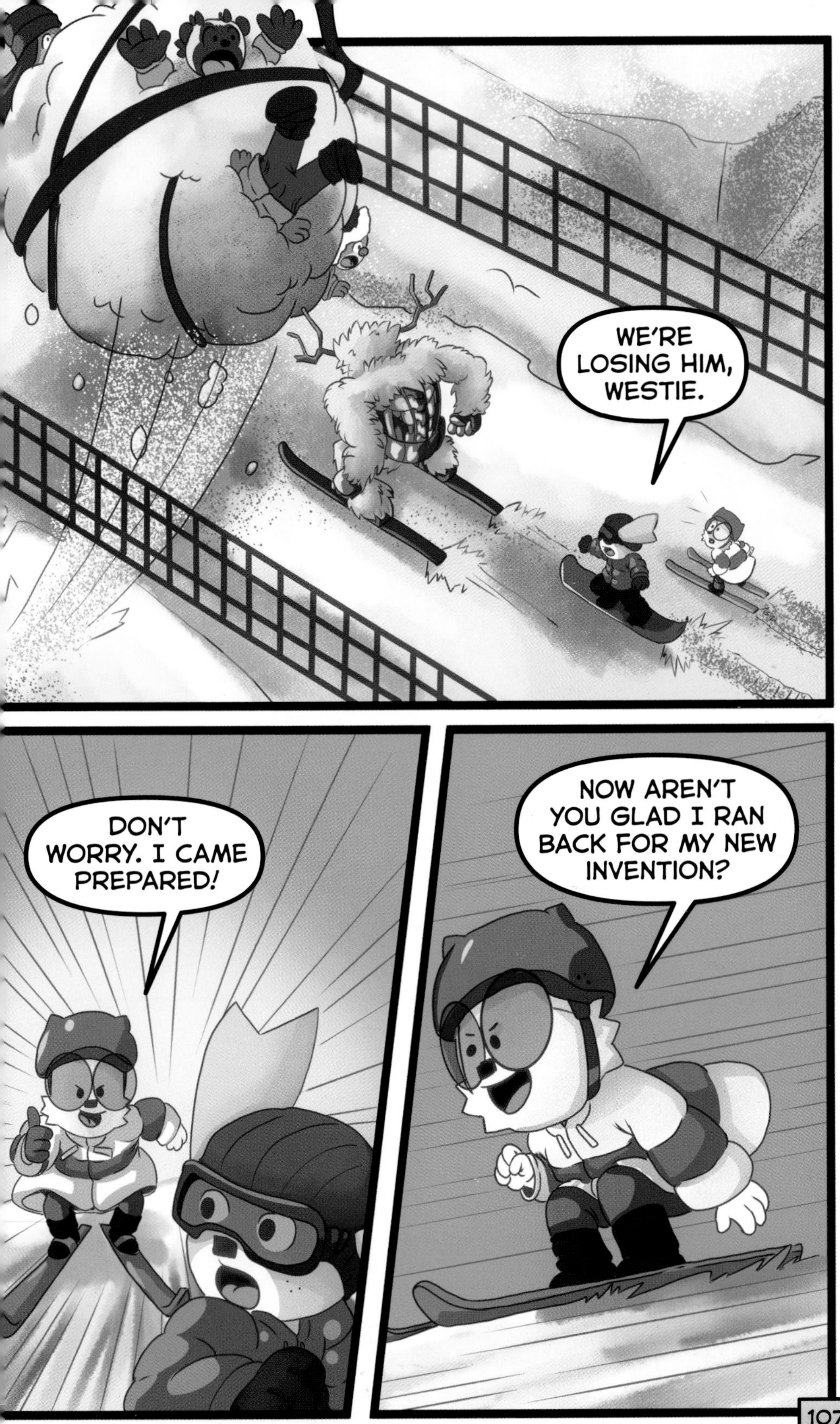
WE'RE LOSING HIM, WESTIE.
DON'T WORRY. I CAME PREPARED!
NOW AREN'T YOU GLAD I RAN BACK FOR MY NEW INVENTION?

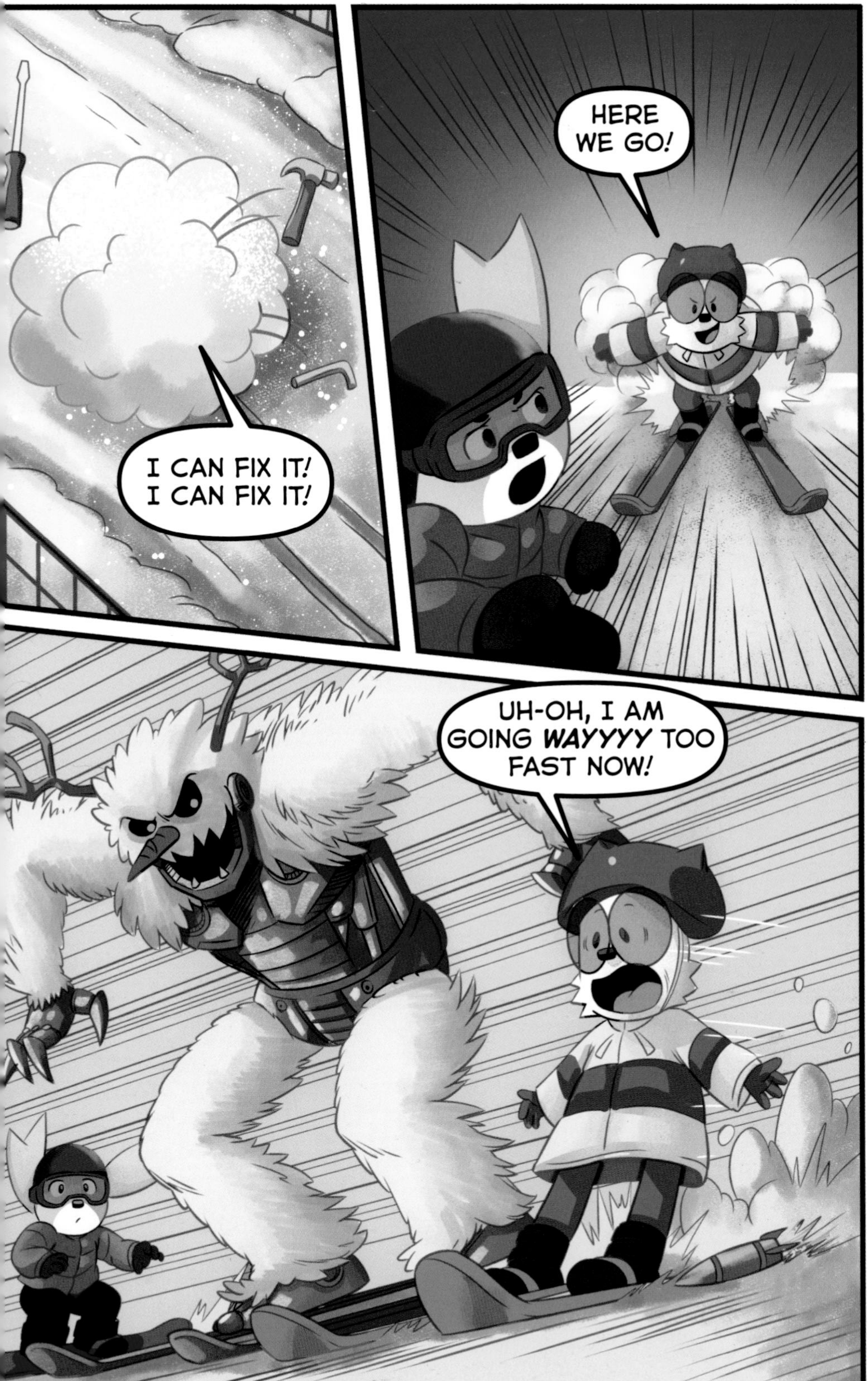
I CAN FIX IT! I CAN FIX IT!
HERE WE GO!
UH-OH, I AM GOING *WAYYYY* TOO FAST NOW!

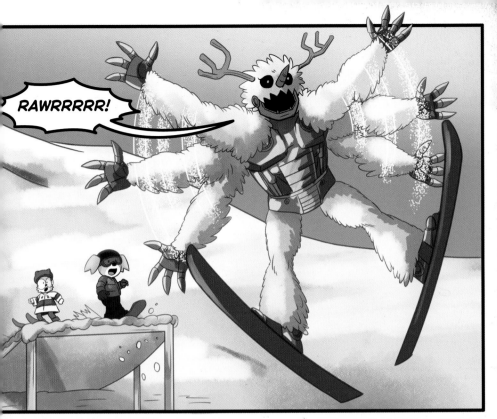

RAWRRRRR!

SPLAT!

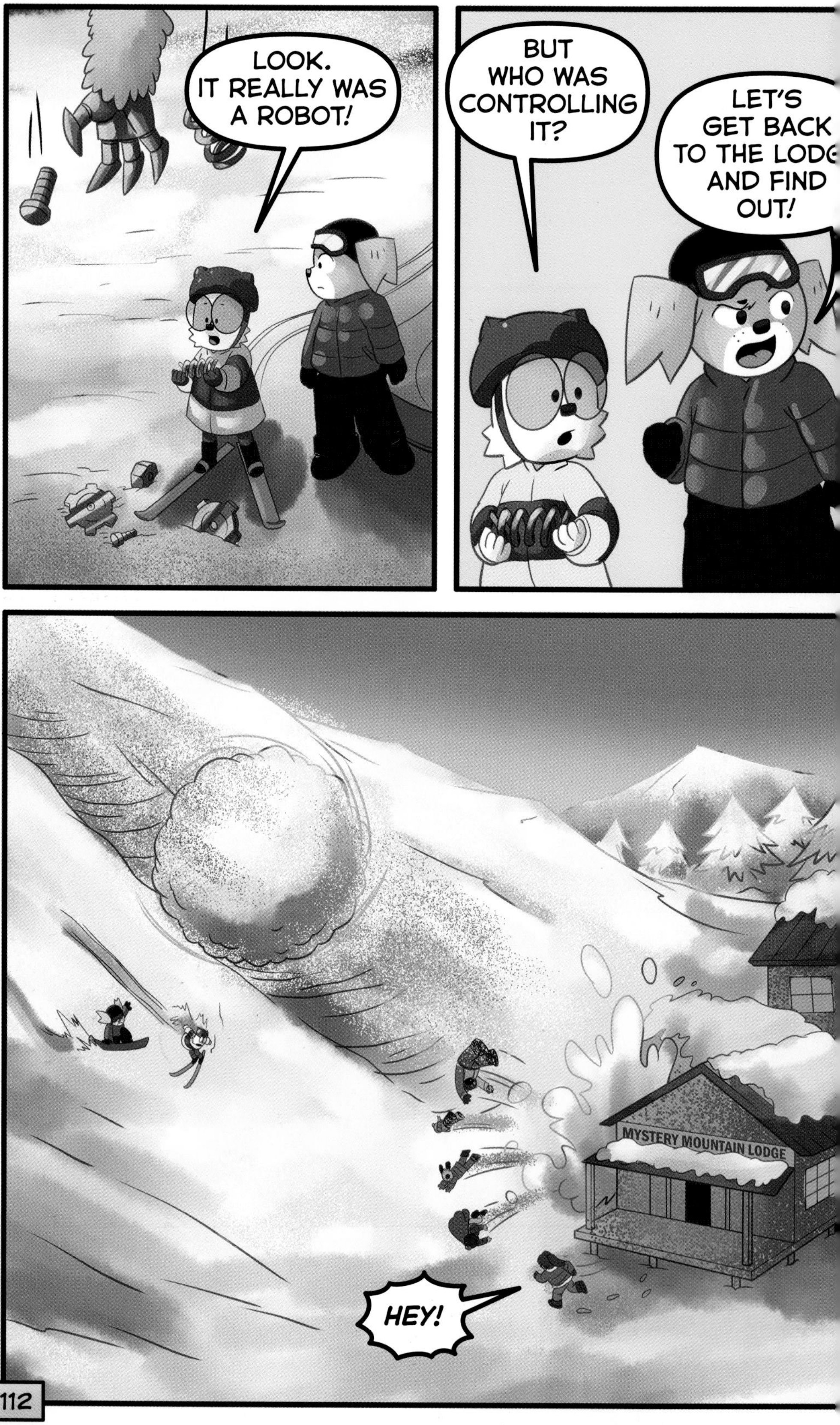
LOOK. IT REALLY WAS A ROBOT!
BUT WHO WAS CONTROLLING IT?
LET'S GET BACK TO THE LODG AND FIND OUT!
MYSTERY MOUNTAIN LODGE
HEY!

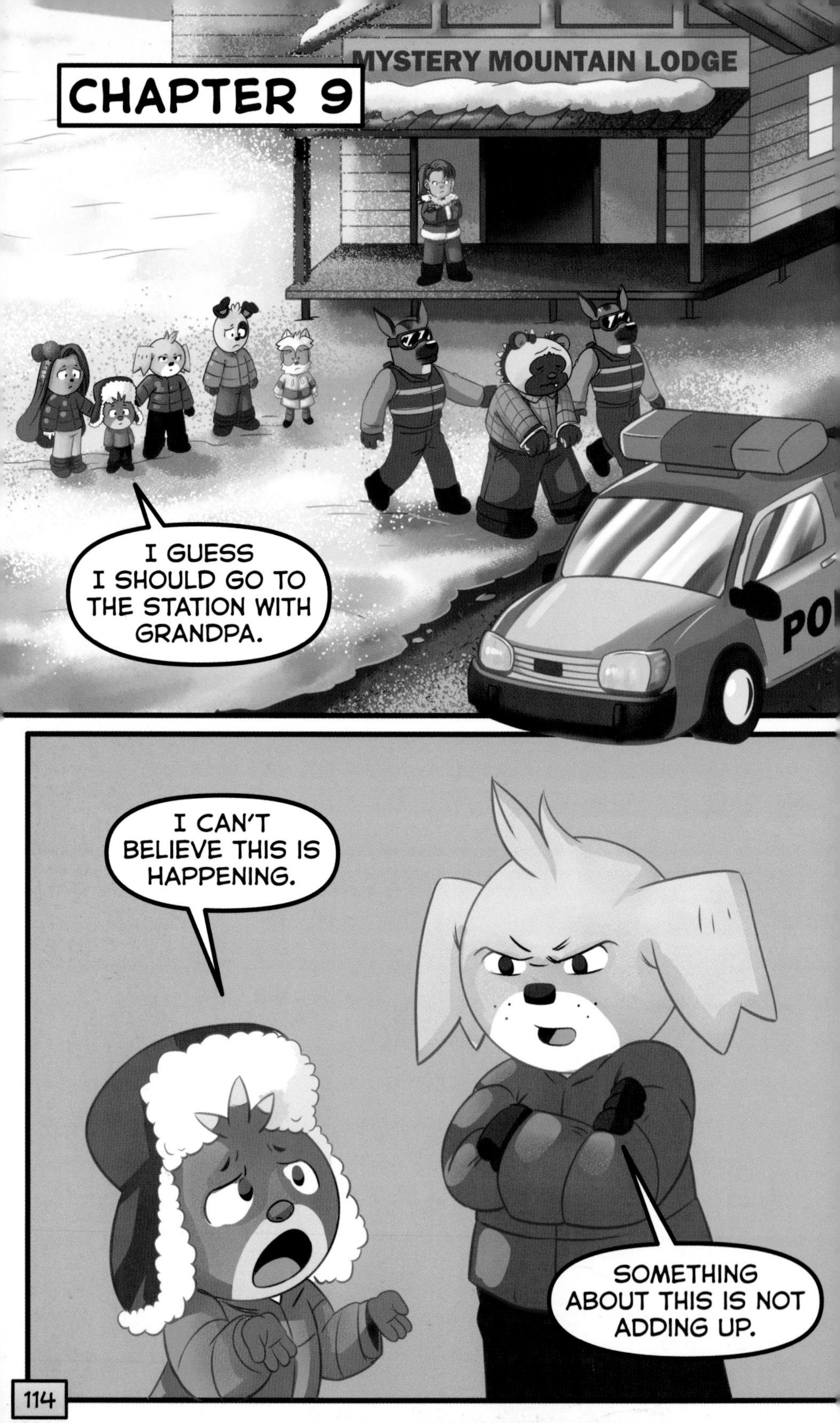
CHAPTER 9
MYSTERY MOUNTAIN LODGE
I GUESS I SHOULD GO TO THE STATION WITH GRANDPA.
PO
I CAN'T BELIEVE THIS IS HAPPENING.
SOMETHING ABOUT THIS IS NOT ADDING UP.

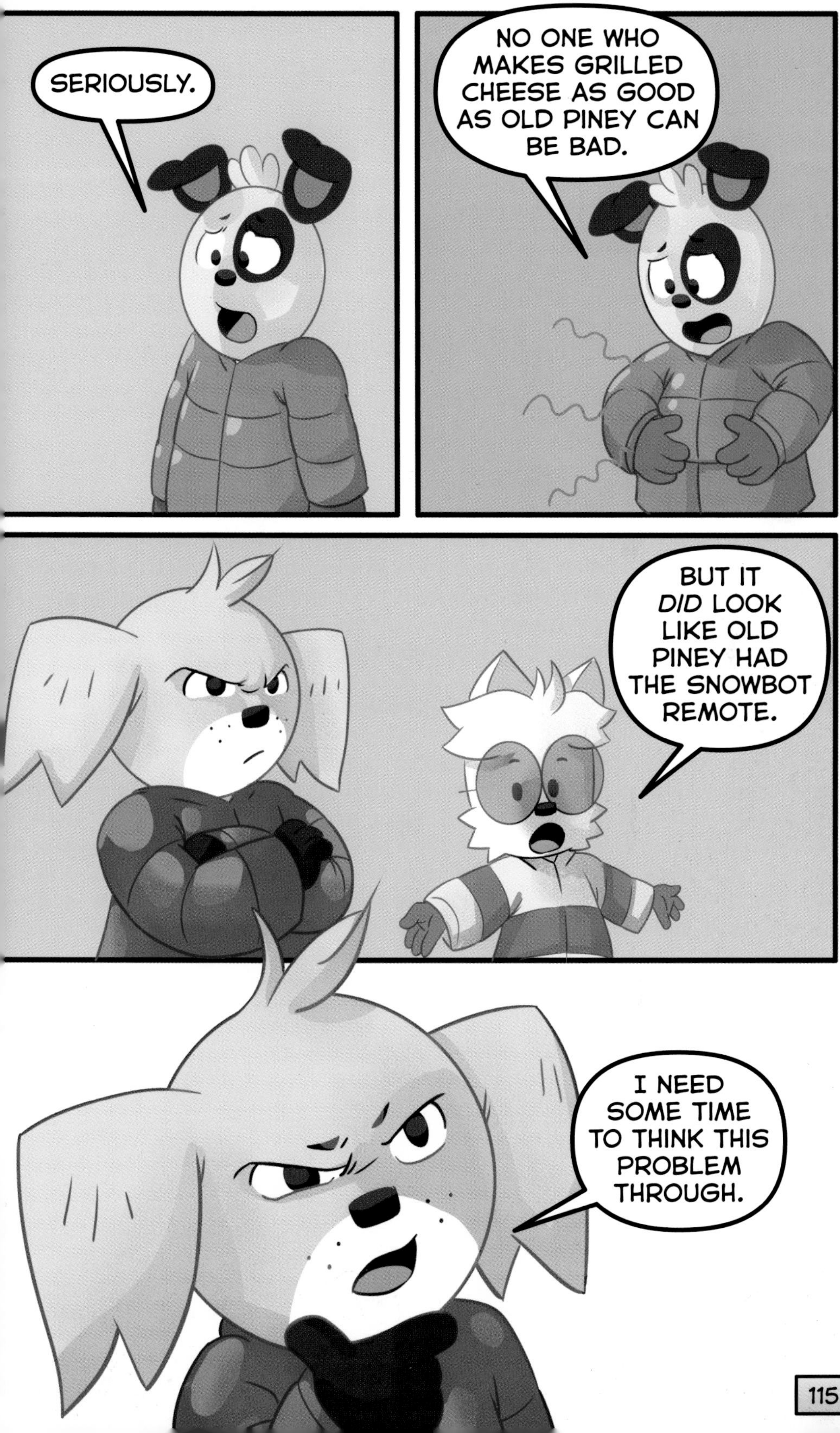
SERIOUSLY.
NO ONE WHO MAKES GRILLED CHEESE AS GOOD AS OLD PINEY CAN BE BAD.
BUT IT *DID* LOOK LIKE OLD PINEY HAD THE SNOWBOT REMOTE.
I NEED SOME TIME TO THINK THIS PROBLEM THROUGH.

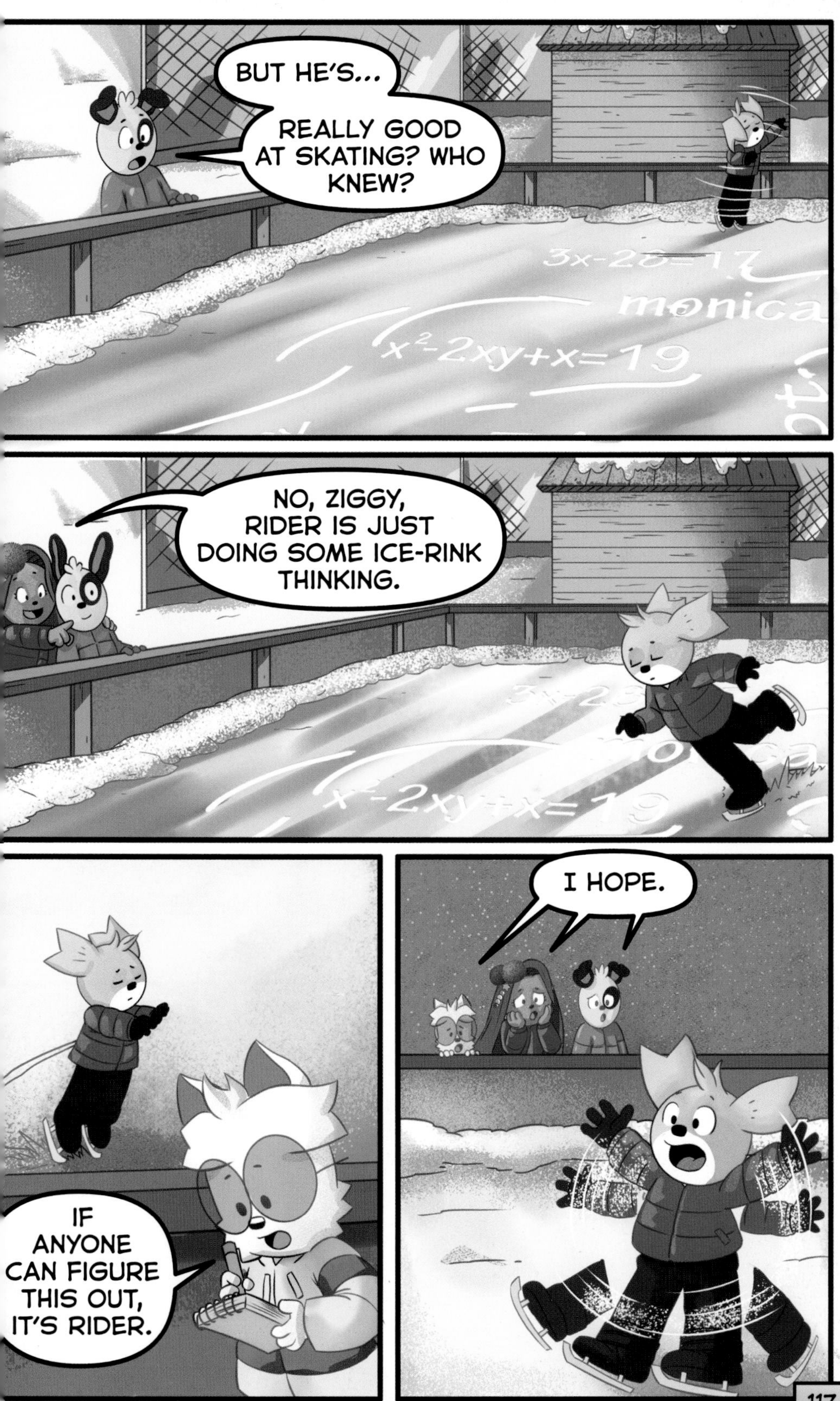
BUT HE'S...
REALLY GOOD AT SKATING? WHO KNEW?
$3x-28=17$
monica
$x^2-2xy+x=19$
NO, ZIGGY, RIDER IS JUST DOING SOME ICE-RINK THINKING.
IF ANYONE CAN FIGURE THIS OUT, IT'S RIDER.
I HOPE.

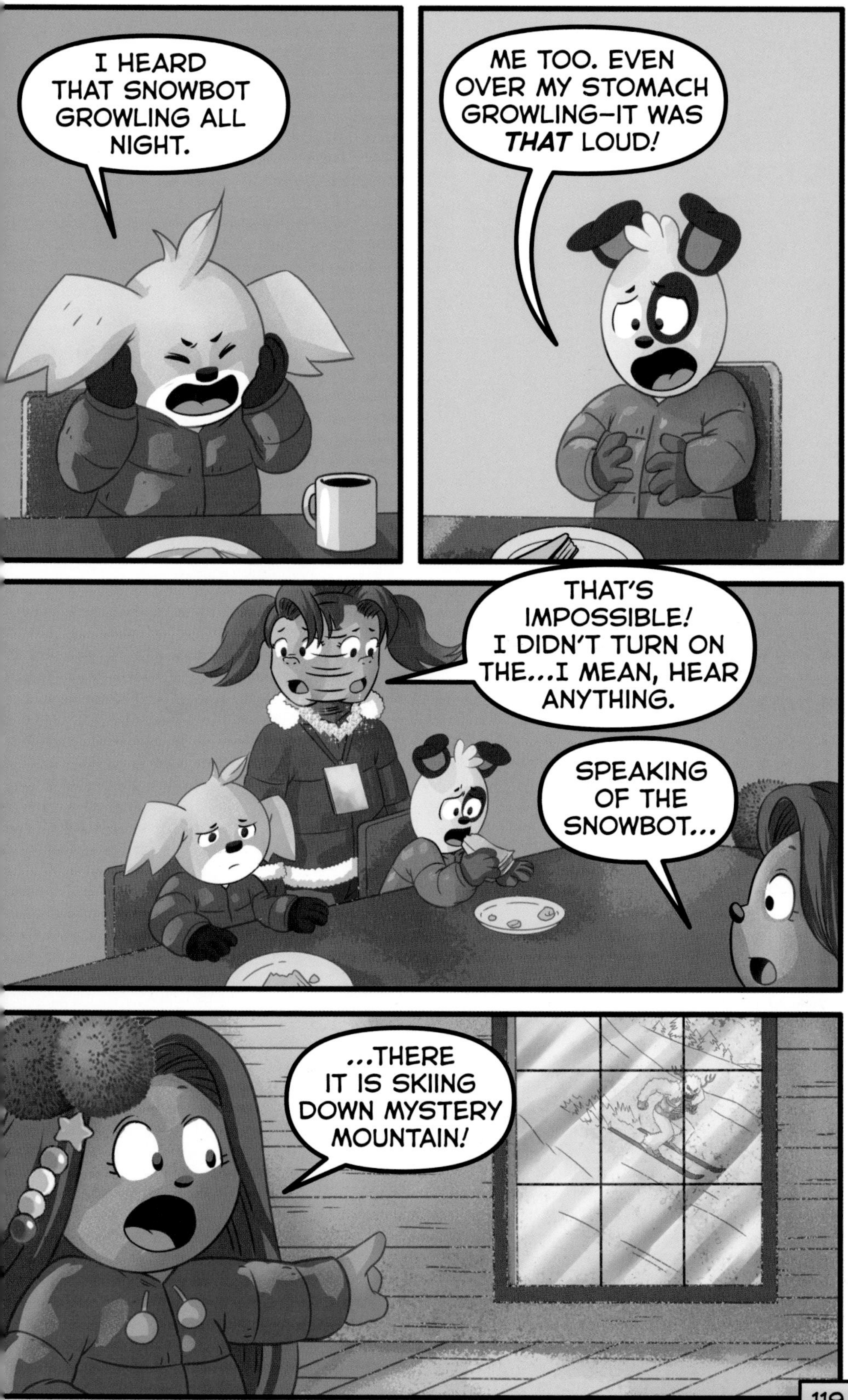
I HEARD THAT SNOWBOT GROWLING ALL NIGHT.
ME TOO. EVEN OVER MY STOMACH GROWLING—IT WAS *THAT* LOUD!
THAT'S IMPOSSIBLE! I DIDN'T TURN ON THE...I MEAN, HEAR ANYTHING.
SPEAKING OF THE SNOWBOT...
...THERE IT IS SKIING DOWN MYSTERY MOUNTAIN!

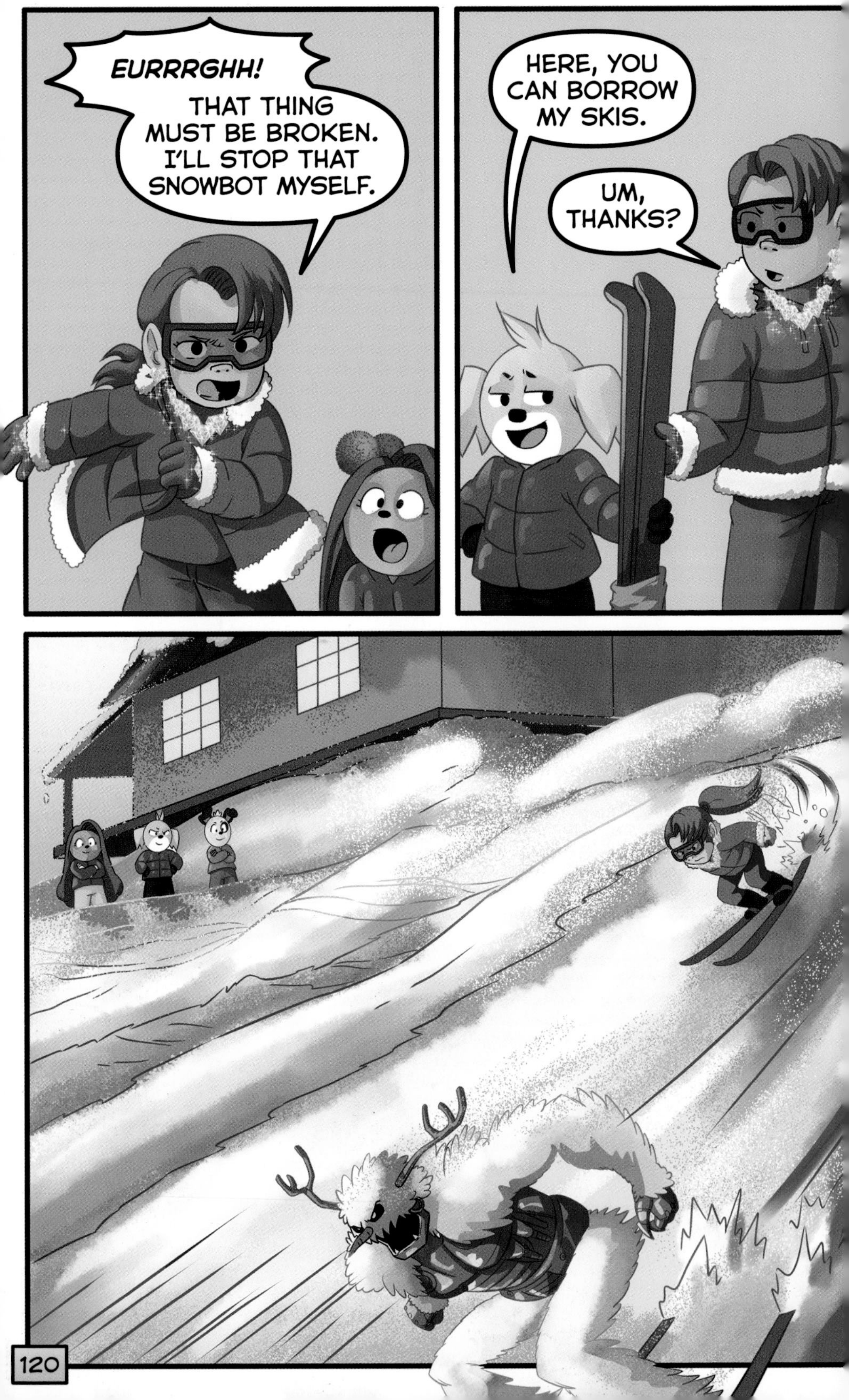
EURRRGHH!
THAT THING MUST BE BROKEN. I'LL STOP THAT SNOWBOT MYSELF.
HERE, YOU CAN BORROW MY SKIS.
UM, THANKS?

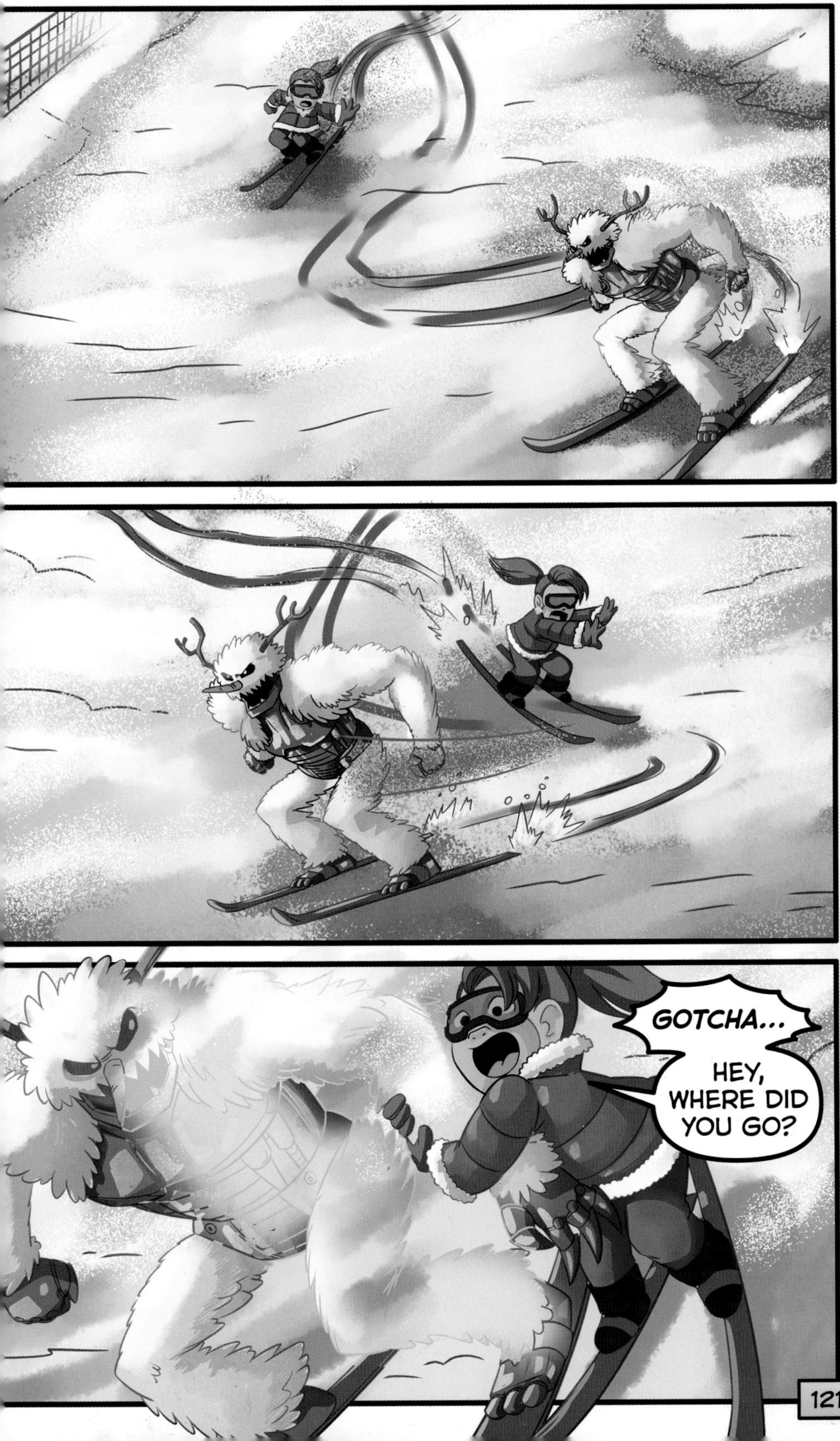
GOTCHA...
HEY, WHERE DID YOU GO?

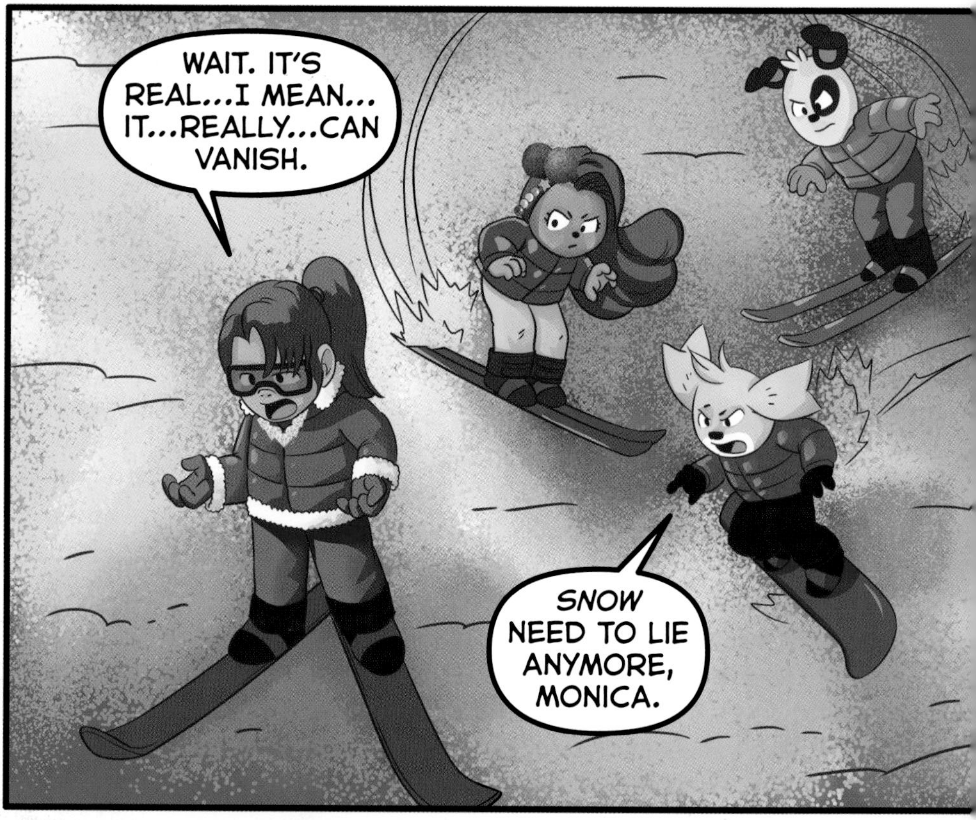
WAIT. IT'S REAL...I MEAN... IT...REALLY...CAN VANISH.
SNOW NEED TO LIE ANYMORE, MONICA.

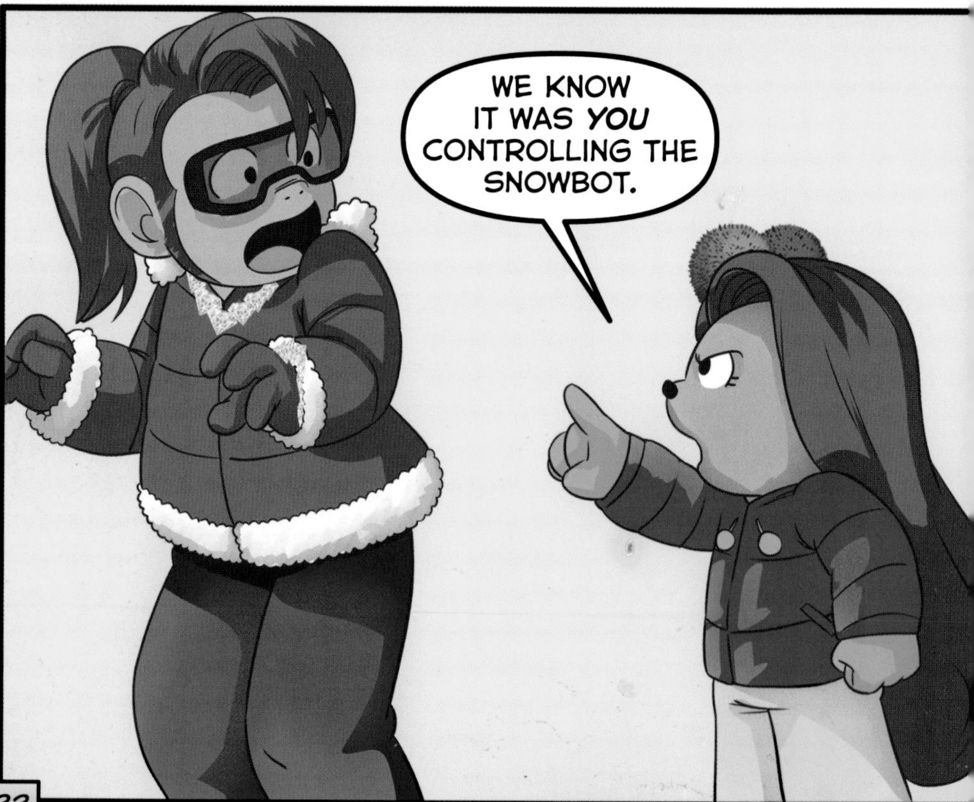
WE KNOW IT WAS *YOU* CONTROLLING THE SNOWBOT.

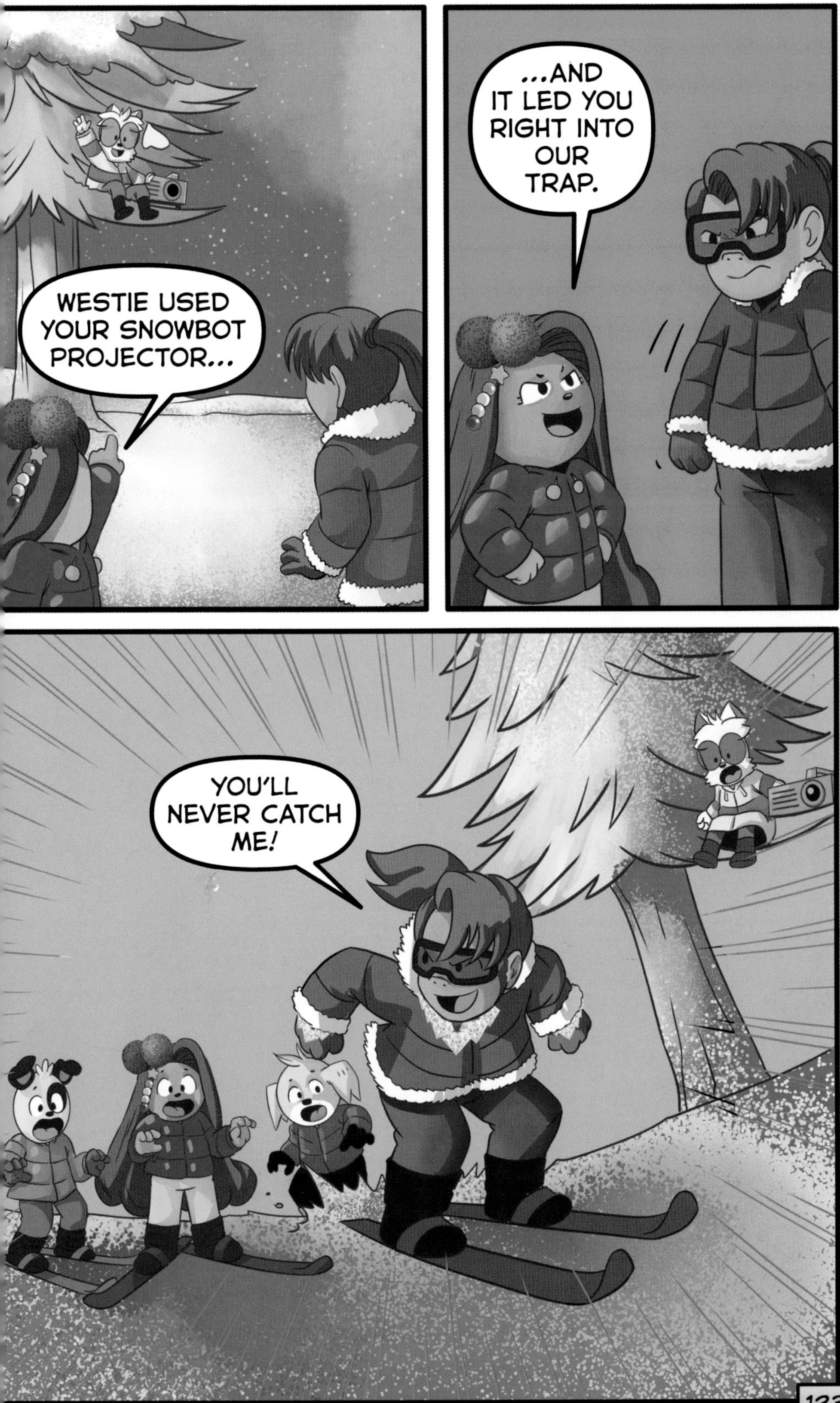
WESTIE USED YOUR SNOWBOT PROJECTOR...
...AND IT LED YOU RIGHT INTO OUR TRAP.
YOU'LL NEVER CATCH ME!

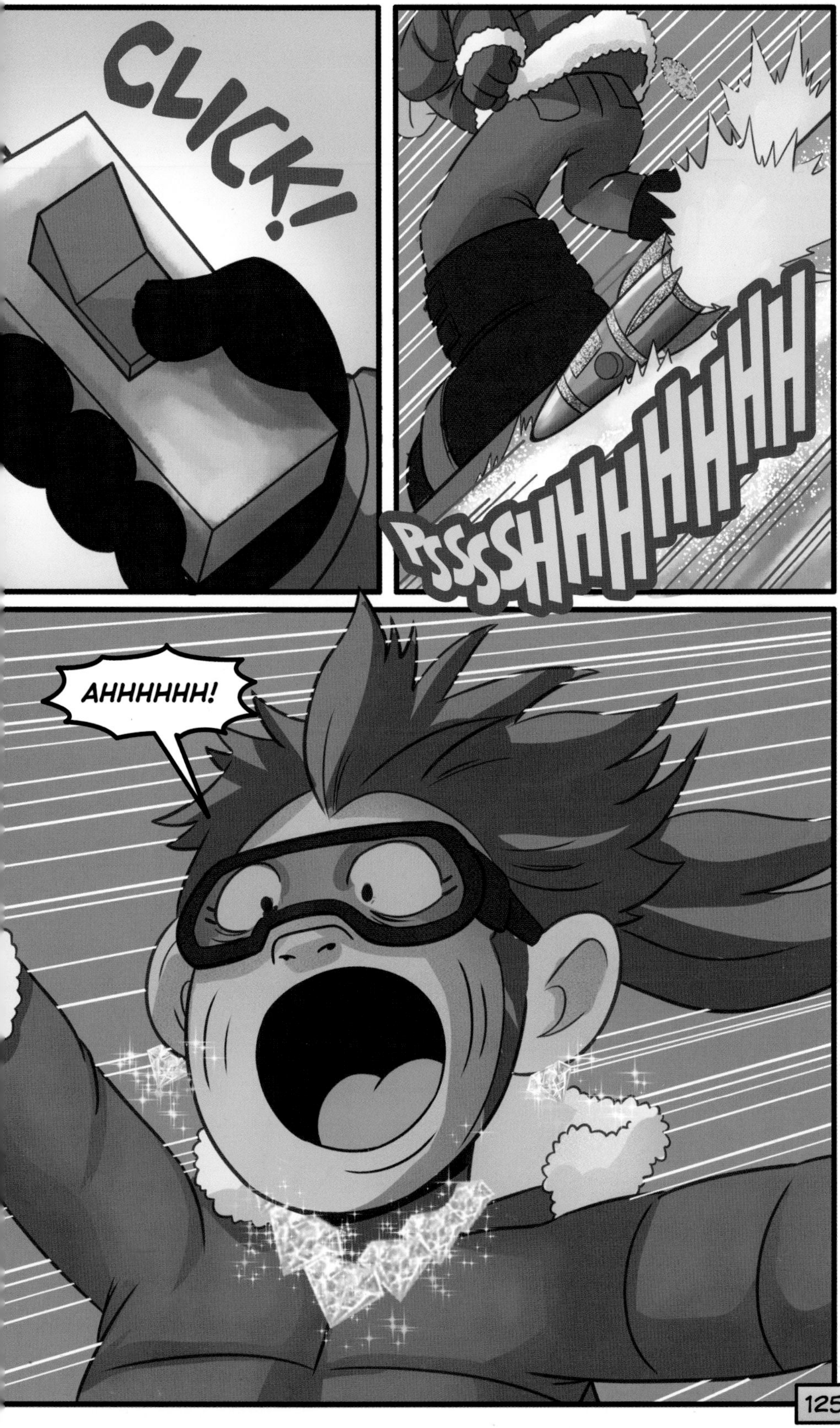
CLICK!
PSSSHHHHHHHHHH
AHHHHHH!

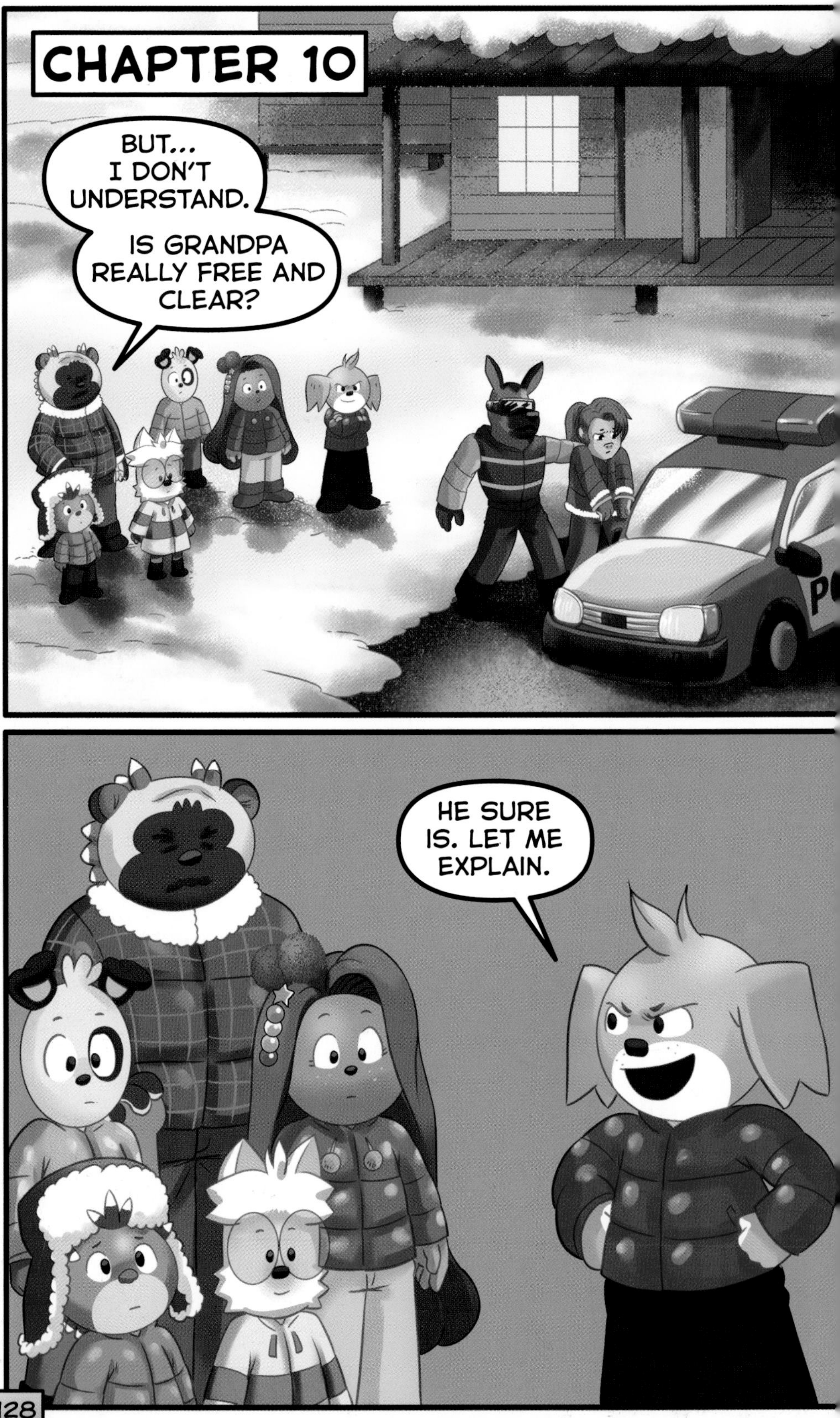
CHAPTER 10
BUT... I DON'T UNDERSTAND.
IS GRANDPA REALLY FREE AND CLEAR?
PO
HE SURE IS. LET ME EXPLAIN.

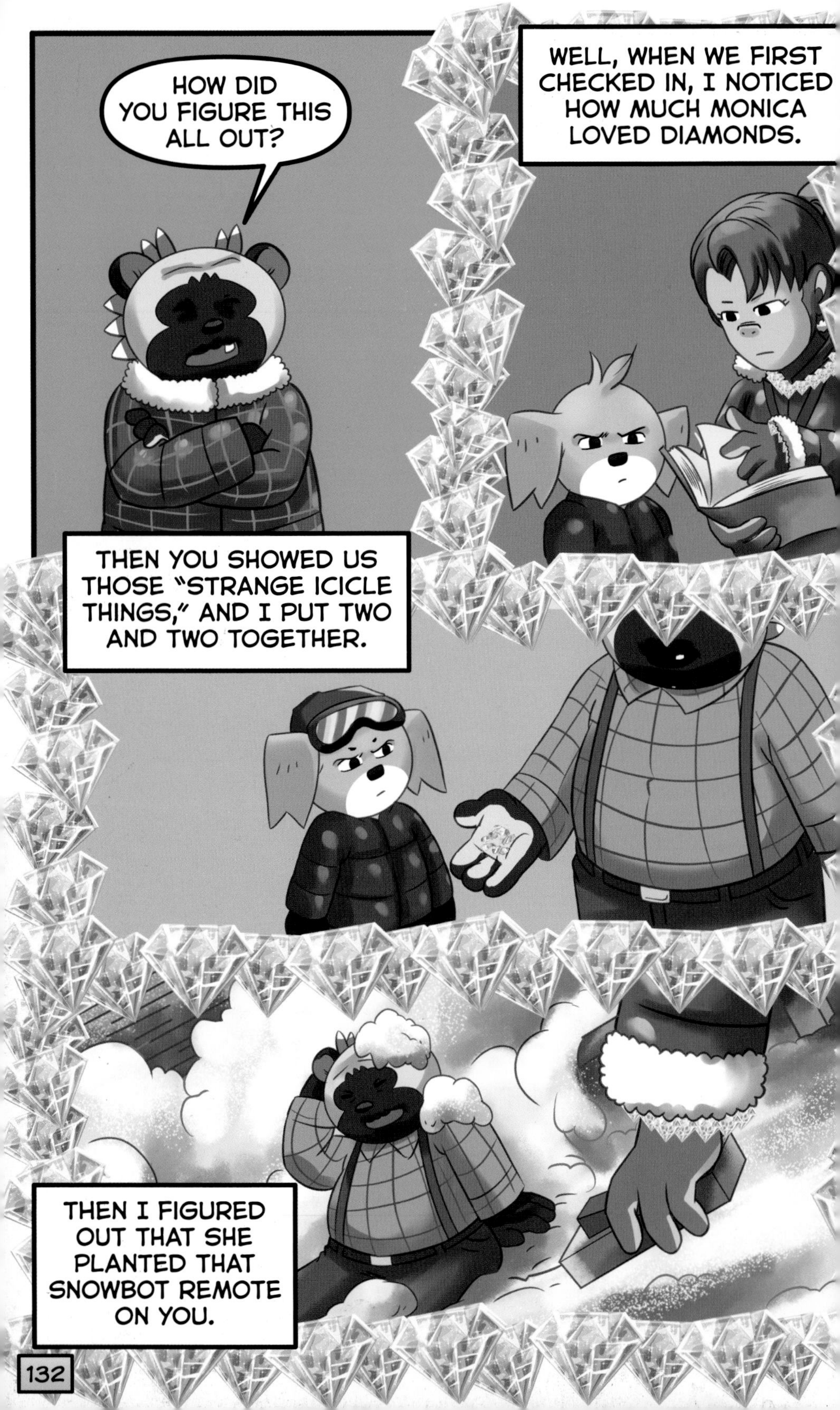
HOW DID YOU FIGURE THIS ALL OUT?
WELL, WHEN WE FIRST CHECKED IN, I NOTICED HOW MUCH MONICA LOVED DIAMONDS.
THEN YOU SHOWED US THOSE "STRANGE ICICLE THINGS," AND I PUT TWO AND TWO TOGETHER.
THEN I FIGURED OUT THAT SHE PLANTED THAT SNOWBOT REMOTE ON YOU.

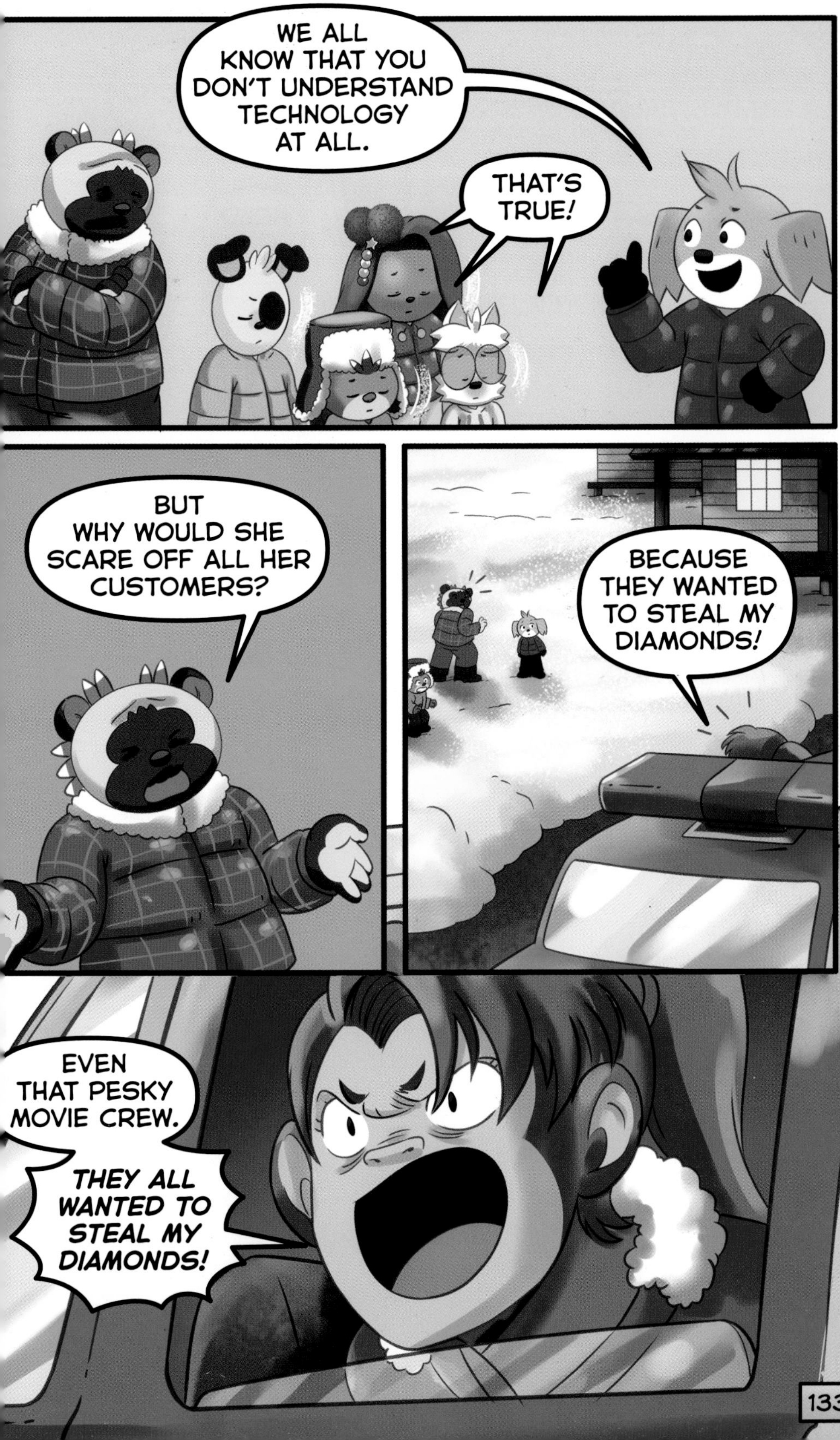
WE ALL KNOW THAT YOU DON'T UNDERSTAND TECHNOLOGY AT ALL.
THAT'S TRUE!
BUT WHY WOULD SHE SCARE OFF ALL HER CUSTOMERS?
BECAUSE THEY WANTED TO STEAL MY DIAMONDS!
EVEN THAT PESKY MOVIE CREW.
THEY ALL WANTED TO STEAL MY DIAMONDS!

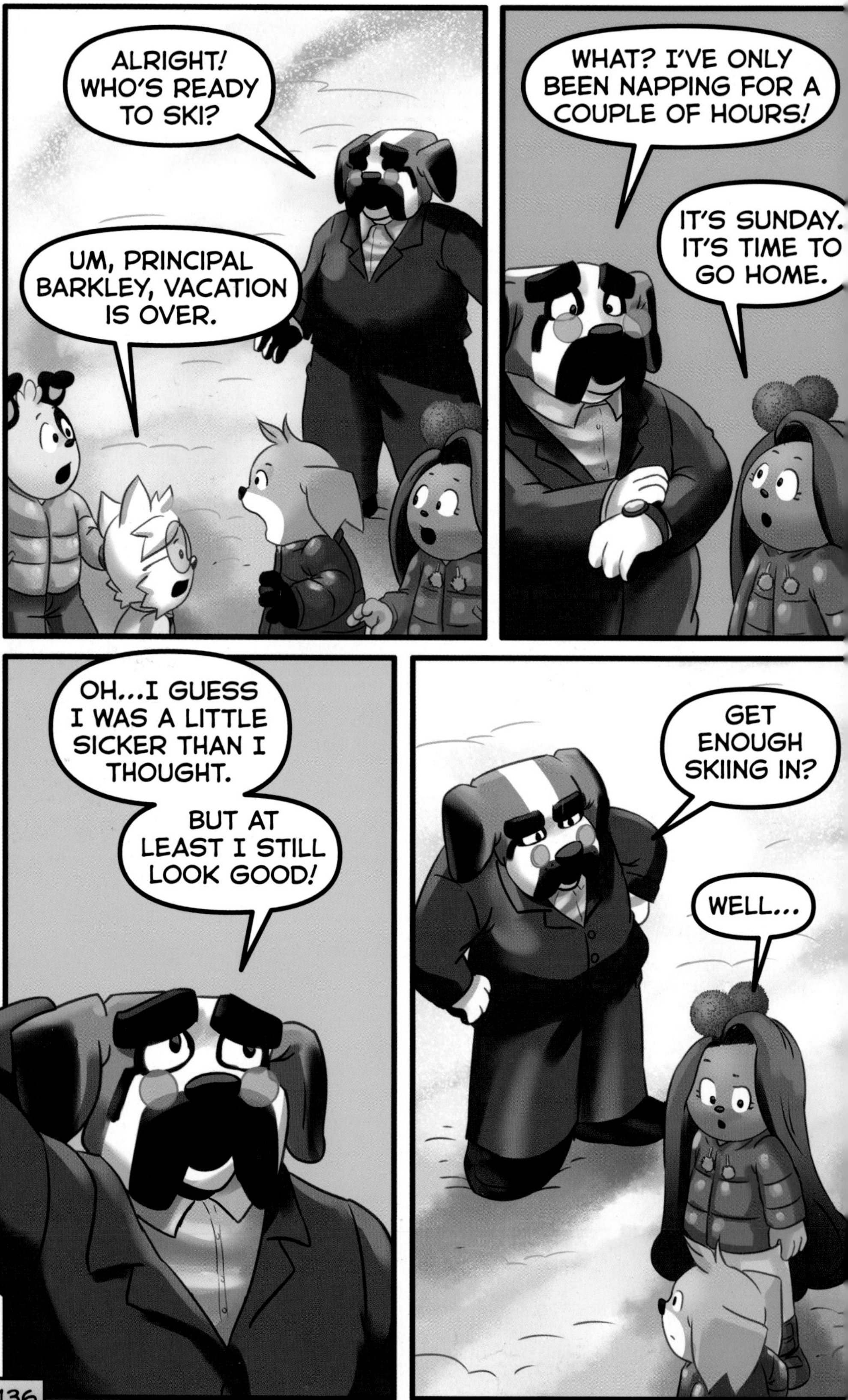
ALRIGHT! WHO'S READY TO SKI?
UM, PRINCIPAL BARKLEY, VACATION IS OVER.
WHAT? I'VE ONLY BEEN NAPPING FOR A COUPLE OF HOURS!
IT'S SUNDAY. IT'S TIME TO GO HOME.
OH...I GUESS I WAS A LITTLE SICKER THAN I THOUGHT.
BUT AT LEAST I STILL LOOK GOOD!
GET ENOUGH SKIING IN?
WELL...

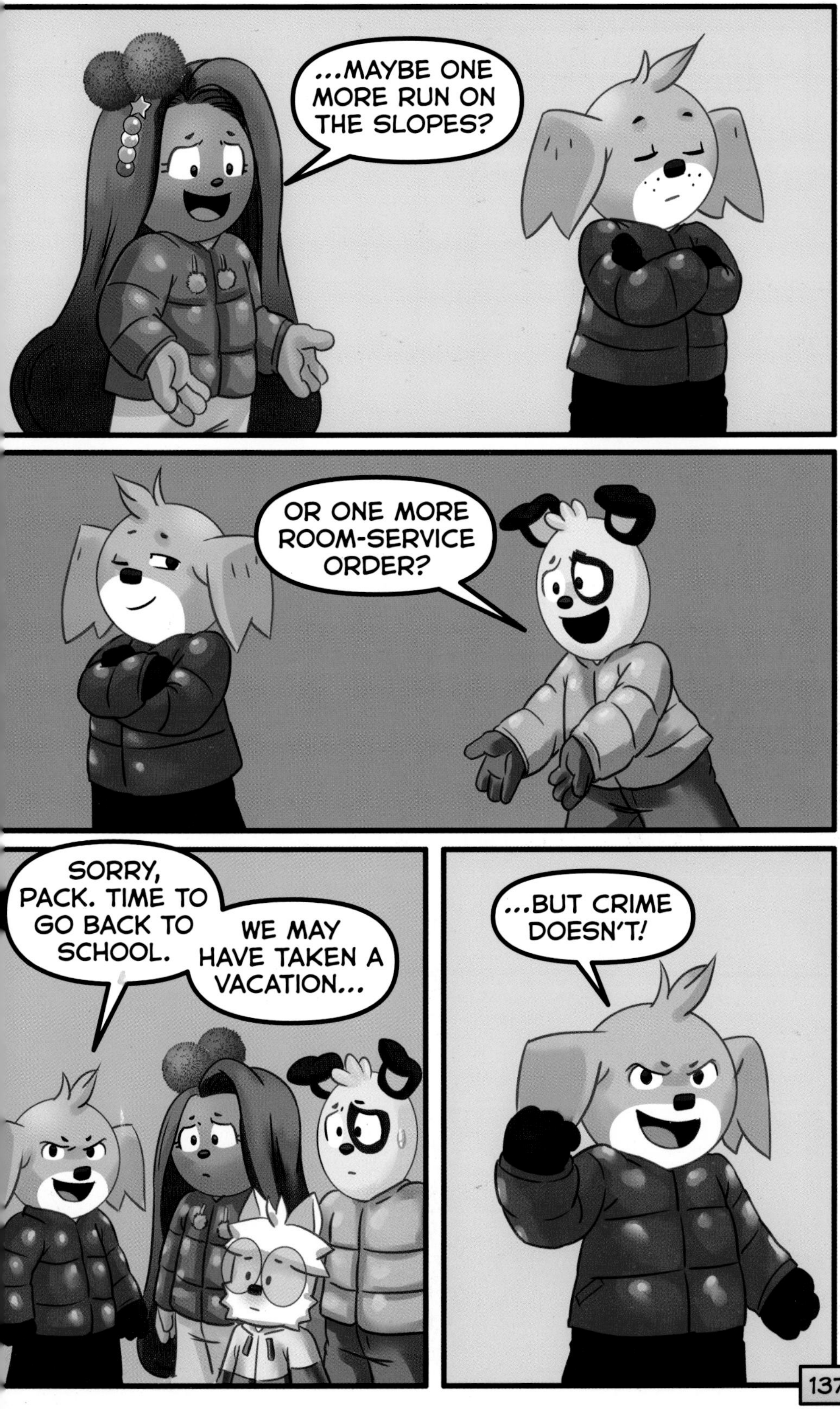
...MAYBE ONE MORE RUN ON THE SLOPES?
OR ONE MORE ROOM-SERVICE ORDER?
SORRY, PACK. TIME TO GO BACK TO SCHOOL.
WE MAY HAVE TAKEN A VACATION...
...BUT CRIME DOESN'T!

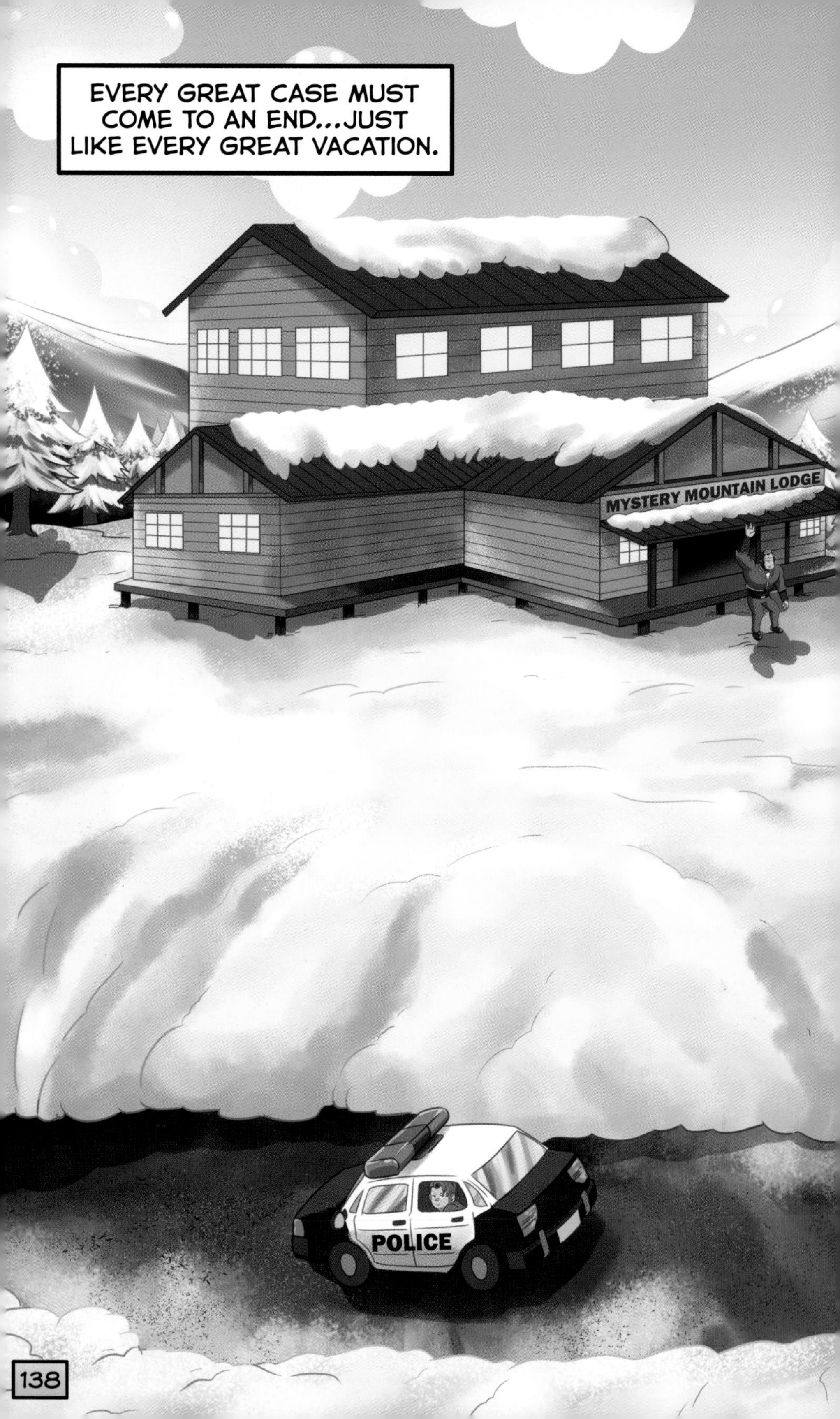
EVERY GREAT CASE MUST COME TO AN END...JUST LIKE EVERY GREAT VACATION.
MYSTERY MOUNTAIN LODGE
POLICE

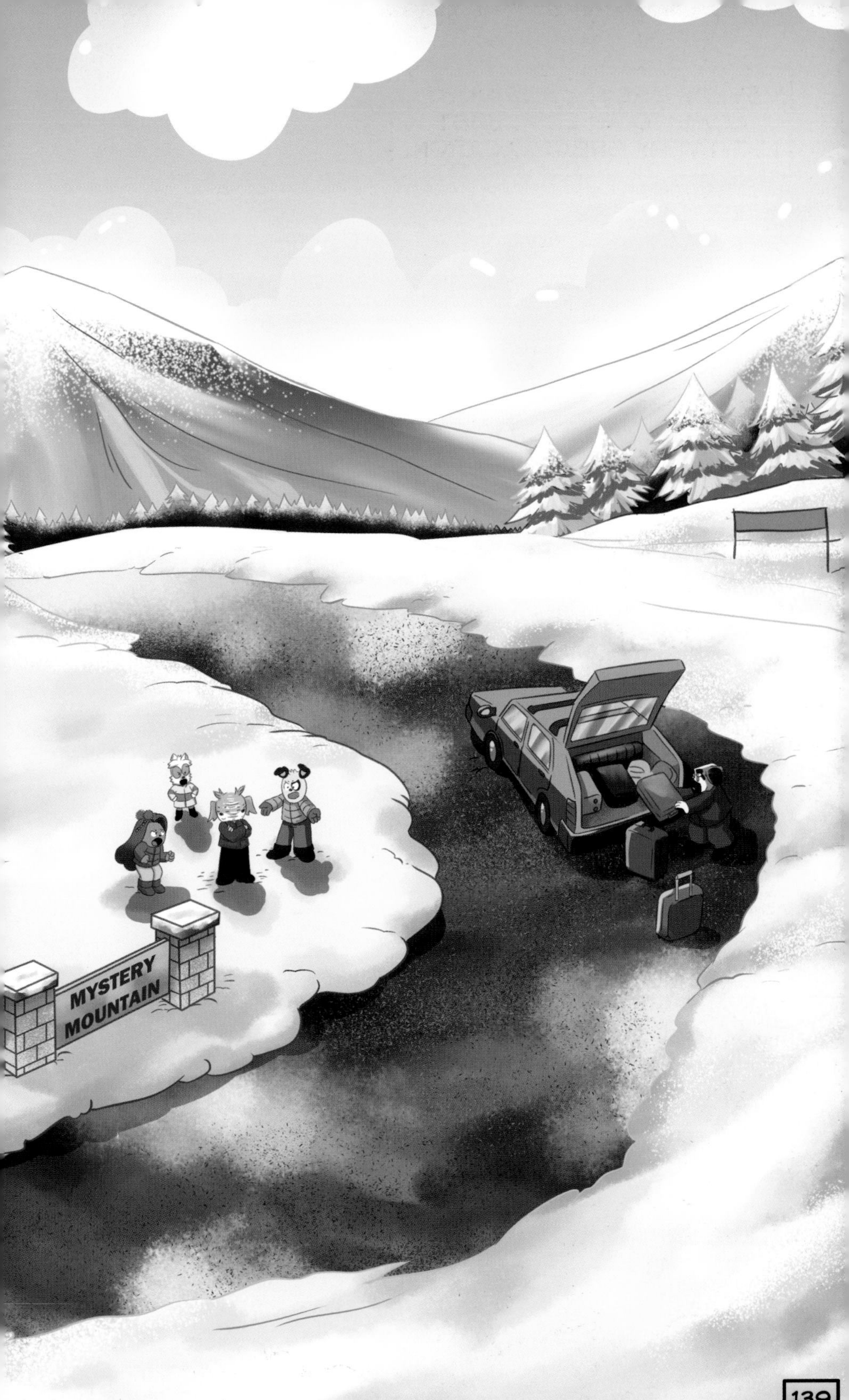
MYSTERY
MOUNTAIN

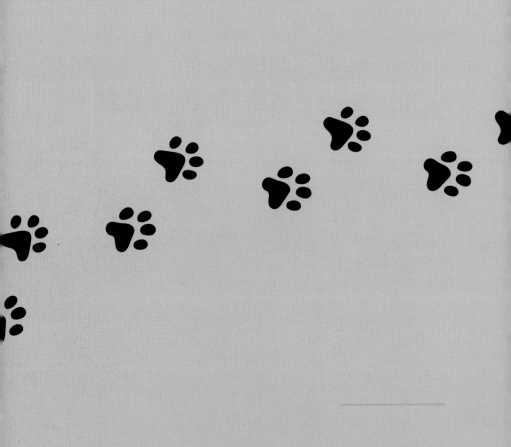

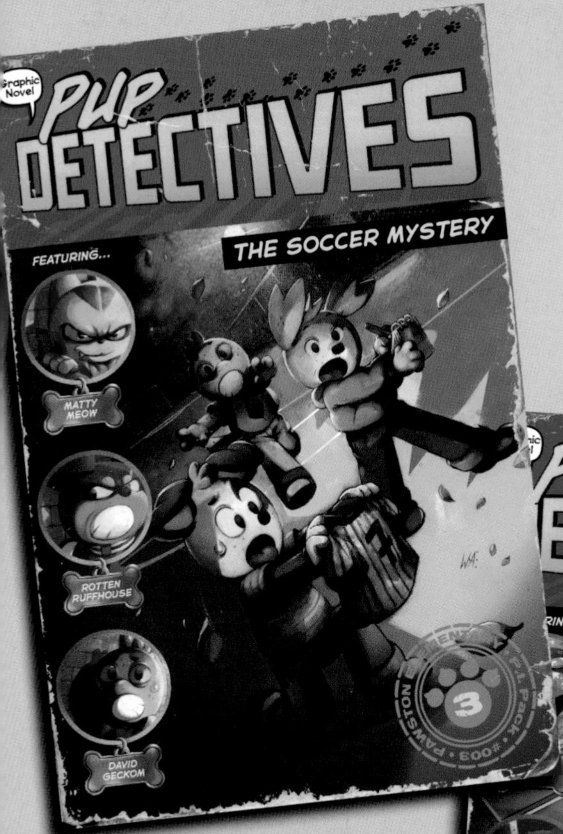
Graphic Novel
PUP DETECTIVES
THE SOCCER MYSTERY
FEATURING...
MATTY MEOW
ROTTEN RUFFHOUSE
DAVID GECKOM
3
#003

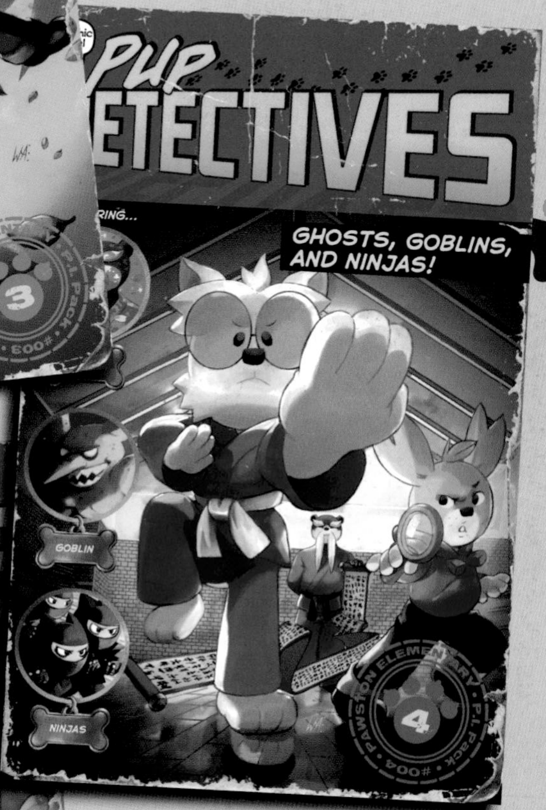
GHOSTS, GOBLINS, AND NINJAS!
GOBLIN
NINJAS
PAWSTON ELEMENTARY P.I. Pack
4
#004

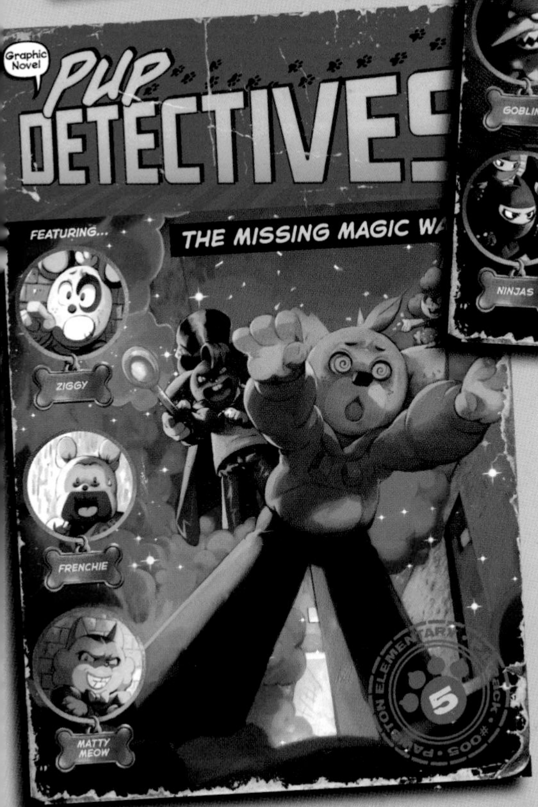
Graphic Novel
FEATURING...
ZIGGY
FRENCHIE
MATTY MEOW
5
#005